THE DOLL

'Phyllis, where the hell have you been? I've been looking all over for you!'

She could find no words. She just sat there staring at him, her eyes wide with astonishment.

'Why didn't you come back to the boat that evening?' he demanded. The questions were tumbling out. 'Did I offend you in some way? Didn't you want to see me again?'

'No. I did want to see you again,' she cut in, recovering herself. 'I intended to come back, but – Peter, please leave me alone! Stop the taxi!'

'He ignored the pleading in her voice, took hold of her arm. 'You've got to tell me what this is all about. I want to know why you lied to me, why you suddenly disappeared –'

At that moment the taxi took a sudden lurch towards the kerb and stopped with a jerk. Phyllis was half out before he managed to grab her by the arm.

Phyllis, listen to me!'

'Let go of my arm!'

'Not till you've told me what this is all about.' He tightened his grip.

'I can't tell you. Peter, please! *Leave me alone*!'

**Also by the same author,
and available in Coronet Books:**

Breakaway

The Doll

Francis Durbridge

CORONET BOOKS
Hodder and Stoughton

Copyright © 1982 by Serial Productions Ltd.

First published in Great Britain 1982 by Hodder and
Stoughton Ltd

Coronet edition 1984

British Library C.I.P.

Durbridge, Francis
  The doll.
  I. Title
  823'.912[F]   PR6054.U7

  ISBN 0-340-34912-3

Printed and bound in Great Britain for
Hodder and Stoughton Paperbacks, a
division of Hodder and Stoughton Ltd.,
Mill Road, Dunton Green, Sevenoaks,
Kent (Editorial Office: 47 Bedford
Square, London, WC1 3DP) by
Cox & Wyman Ltd., Reading

1

Taking authors out to lunch was an important part of Peter Matty's job as a publisher of books. He had found a new restaurant near the British Museum and decided to try it out on the author of a very promising first novel. It was not until they had finished their meal and were leaving that he spotted the girl sitting with her back to them three tables away. It was her magnificent auburn hair that misled him. He impulsively went towards her. When he was within a few feet she turned her head and he saw that her profile bore no resemblance to Phyllis.

After saying goodbye to his author he decided to walk back to the office rather than take a taxi. It would clear his head for the work of the afternoon and give him a chance to get his thoughts sorted out. Just for a moment he thought he'd at last found the girl who had vanished so suddenly and so inexplicably from his life.

His mind was far away as he walked through Russell Square. It was a sunny afternoon and the spring leaves were casting moving shadows on the pavement. It was even possible to hear the sparrows when the traffic slackened a little.

He stepped off the pavement to cross the street. Immediately there was a squeal of brakes and tyres from behind him. A delivery van careered past within inches. The driver's scared and angry shout brought him to his senses. He regained the pavement to a chorus of horn-blasts. His heart was beating rapidly. He stared at the rear of the receding van, grateful for the driver's quick reflexes. That sort of thing had been happening far too often lately. He realised that if he went on like this his expectation of life would not be very high.

This time he waited, checking the traffic coming from both directions before venturing out into the road once more. Opposite him was an elegant three-storey house with bow windows and a front door flanked by two columns and topped by a fanlight. The brickwork had been recently repointed. The brass plate at the side of the door discreetly informed the visitor that this was the home of Peter's two companies: Matty Books Ltd. and Matty Paperbacks Ltd.

As he crossed the pavement and approached the two steps that led to the front door a uniformed messenger emerged with a sheaf of envelopes and flat packages under his arm. He directed a respectful salute at the well-dressed man in the light overcoat.

'Afternoon, Mr Matty.'

Peter started. He seemed to have difficulty in recognising his own name. He gazed blankly at the messenger.

'Oh. Good afternoon, Henry.'

The messenger, whose real name was Harold, stared after him as he disappeared into the building, then shook his head and went on his way.

Mollie Stafford, Peter's secretary, had a small office on the first floor. Any visitor had to pass through it to gain access to Peter's own office, which looked out over the street and gave a glimpse of the trees in the square. She was an attractive girl with a good figure. That did not stop her from being extremely efficient. She always wore large spectacles when in the office. They gave her a more studious and academic look but appeared to offer no magnification. Peter often wondered if she used them merely for effect. It was easy to tell when Mollie was around. She was very fond of bracelets and necklaces which jingled whenever she moved. If she had a fault it was a tendency to be excitable.

At the moment when Peter was having his brush with death in the street outside she was grappling with the incoming calls on two different telephones.

'No, I'm afraid you can't. Mr Matty isn't back from lunch yet . . . I'm sorry, I don't know when he will be in the office . . . Yes, *of course* I'm expecting him . . . Yes, please do that. Thank you for calling.'

She put the receiver down with a sigh and picked up the other phone which was lying on the desk.

'Sorry about that, Mr Walters. Look, it's just occurred to me. Mr Matty probably sent your proofs to someone else . . . Well—I'm afraid he has been doing some very odd things just lately . . . Anyway, not to worry, I'll send you another set . . . Yes, of course. Leave it to me.'

She had just replaced the receiver and was scribbling a note on her pad when Peter entered. He had that vague, somewhat lost look that she had come to know so well in the past three weeks.

Peter Matty was in his late thirties. He was dark and good-looking and wore his clothes well. Mollie thought he was just what a publisher should be—well-read, idealistic and inclined to be a dreamer. Until recently he had been able to combine those qualities with a sound business sense. Her feelings towards him were protective rather then romantic. She knew very well that he would be at a complete loss without her. All the same, she thought she knew the reason for his present vagueness and she could not help feeling a small twinge of jealousy.

'Oh, good afternoon, Mr Matty,' she greeted him, her face showing relief at his return. 'Am I glad to see you!'

'Hello, Mollie.' Peter's voice was disinterested. He seemed unaware that his late return might have caused problems. 'Any messages?'

'You must be joking!' Mollie exclaimed, laughing. She tore several pages off her pad and handed them to him. 'Try these for starters. And your brother's waiting to see you.'

Peter froze, his hand outstretched for the messages. 'Claude?'

'Yes. He arrived about half an hour ago.'

'But Claude's in Stockholm. He's playing there this evening.'

Mollie shook her head emphatically. The beads of her necklace tinkled. 'He's in your office. The concert's been cancelled.'

Still disbelieving, Peter took the messages and moved to the door of his office. It opened into a large, airy room. There were shelves round three of the walls, stocked with the books published under his imprint since he had set up his own two companies. Peter did not like office furniture. He found it too impersonal. His office was furnished with pieces intended for private houses. As a result it had the appearance more of a den or study.

As he entered, his visitor rose from one of the comfortable easy-chairs. A stranger would not easily have seen a family resemblance between the two brothers. Claude was slightly younger. He was several inches taller than Peter. Whereas Peter was dark, he was fair. His hair, though long, had been expertly cut and enhanced his distinguished appearance. His face was sensitive and expressive. He had the strong, practical hands of a professional pianist. His clothes were informal but elegant, purchased in the different capitals which he visited on his concert tours. Today he was wearing a soft suede jacket from Rome, leather shoes from Zurich, slacks from Frankfurt and a shirt from New York.

He put down the copy of *Publishers Weekly* he had been reading, and gave his brother a quick, assessing look in which there was a measure of concern. 'Hello, Peter. How are you, dear boy?'

Peter came forward and took his brother's right hand in both of his.

'Claude, I thought you were in Stockholm! I couldn't believe it when Mollie said you were here.'

'The concert was cancelled,' Claude said, his faint smile showing his pleasure at his brother's warm welcome.

'Oh, why was that?'

'The conductor, an Italian called Enrico Muralto, was in some sort of trouble and the poor devil suddenly decided to commit suicide.'

'Oh, my God!' Peter relinquished his hold of Claude's hand.

'It was a nasty business. I felt terribly sorry for his wife. She's a delightful woman.'

Peter took his coat off and moved to hang it up on a hook behind the door.

'Well, I must say it's nice to see you, Claude. It really is.' He turned to give his brother a more leisurely inspection. 'And you look fine, in spite of everything.'

'I'm all right. A little tired, perhaps.'

'Yes, I can see that. But it's not surprising. You work yourself too hard. Where's your next recital?'

'San Francisco. But it's not for six weeks, thank goodness.'

'Six weeks. That's quite a break.'

'Yes, it is. And I'm looking forward to it. I haven't had a holiday—a real holiday—for years.'

'I know you haven't. What are you going to do? Pop down to the South of France?'

Claude sat down in the easy chair again and crossed his long legs.

'No, I rather fancy staying in England. For part of the time, at any rate.' He looked up quizzically at Peter. 'I thought I might even seek sanctuary on that boat of yours. If that's all right with you, of course?'

'You know it is! I think that's a splendid idea.'

Claude watched Peter as he took a fresh packet of cigarettes from his pocket, ripped off the cellophane packaging and the strip of silver paper. His movements were quick and nervous, as though it was urgent and important for him to have a cigarette without delay.

'You've lost weight since I saw you.'

'Have I?' Peter looked down at his waist, patted his remarkably flat stomach. 'I don't think so.'

'Yes, you have.'

'Well, perhaps a little.'

Peter threw the cellophane wrapping into the wastepaper basket, and put a cigarette in his mouth. Claude was still watching him with that affectionate but concerned expression.

'Peter, I'm worried. Very worried.'

'About this Italian business?'

'No,' Claude said quietly. 'About you.'

'Me?' Peter paused with the lighter in his hand. 'Good heavens, Claude! Why are you worried about me?'

Claude waited till Peter had lit his cigarette and sat down in the chair facing him.

10

'I've written you four letters in the past fortnight and you haven't replied to any of them. Then when I telephoned you last Sunday morning you sounded vague and confused, almost unfriendly—'

'Unfriendly?' Peter interrupted with a slight frown. 'My dear chap, you're talking nonsense!'

Claude shook his head. 'Quite apart from my own feelings I must have received at least a dozen letters from people in the last ten days. Friends of ours. They all tell exactly the same story. They say you're bad-tempered, morose, and quite obviously worried to death about something.'

Peter drew on his cigarette, keeping his eyes averted from Claude. 'That's ridiculous! Just idle gossip. There's absolutely nothing the matter with me.'

Both men glanced up as the door opened. Mollie came in, carrying a folder of letters for signature and a couple of typescripts. She put them down on Peter's desk, and as she did so glanced once very briefly in the direction of Claude.

'Has Mollie been saying things about me?' Peter demanded, as soon as the door closed on her.

'No, of course not,' Claude said innocently. 'Why should she? You've just told me there's nothing the matter with you.'

'I wondered, that's all.' Peter slumped in his chair, his expression becoming more defensive. 'Well, to be honest, she's been having a tough time just recently. I've been away from the office quite a bit and consequently—'

'Why have you been away from the office? Have you been ill?'

'No. I've told you. I'm perfectly all right. There's nothing for you or anyone else to worry about.'

11

There was a touch of defiance in the way Peter stared back into his brother's steady eyes. It was an expression Claude knew well from the days when they had been schoolboys together.

'Peter, we're going to see a lot of each other during the next couple of weeks. At least, I hope so.'

'I hope so too,' Peter said, without great conviction.

'Then what's this all about?' Claude's voice rose in sudden exasperation. 'I'm going to find out sooner or later, so you might just as well tell me now.'

Although Peter had only smoked a quarter of his cigarette he stubbed it out in the ashtray beside his chair. He stood up and went across to stare out of the window at the traffic passing in the street below. As he showed no inclination to speak, Claude remained silent and sat back to wait.

After a long pause and without turning round Peter said: 'You remember when I flew out to Geneva a few weeks ago to attend your concert?'

'Yes.'

'Well, I don't suppose you remember what happened on the Monday morning?'

'On Monday morning? Didn't I drive you out to the airport?'

'You did. Do you remember the girl who got out of the taxi behind us?'

'Can't say I do.'

'She had too much luggage and was shedding parcels and magazines all over the place—'

'Wait a minute.' Claude half closed his eyes in the effort to recall the scene. 'You mean a tall, attractive woman with auburn hair? Very well dressed?'

'Yes, that's her.'

'The last I saw of you, you were picking up some magazines she'd dropped and were tucking them under her arm.'

Peter nodded. When he turned round Claude saw a rueful smile on his face. 'Well, it wasn't the last I saw of her.'

2

The excuse to fly to Geneva for Claude's concert had been too good an opportunity to miss. Peter had sold the German rights of one of his recent publications to a Swiss paperback firm and he needed to sort out some of the details. As large sums of money were involved he had every justification for arranging a meeting with the Swiss publisher. Besides, it was Claude's first recital in Europe after a tour of the Far East. The brothers had not met for nearly a year.

The concert was a great success and before he left Peter was able to share Claude's pleasure at the excellent notices he received in the following day's papers. Claude drove him out to the airport in the BMW he had hired for his stay in Geneva.

There were the usual parking restrictions outside the Departure entrance. Claude and Peter had already said their goodbyes in the car as they knew there would not be much time at the airport. A Swiss policeman's eye was already on them as Peter got out and Claude went round to the boot to unload his suitcase. A Geneva taxi had drawn up behind the BMW. Peter's attention was attracted by the very good-looking young woman who stepped out. While the driver unloaded her two suitcases she waved imperiously to a porter. A uniformed man quickly stepped forward. The woman turned back to the taxi to collect her belongings from the back seat. She had a number of gift-wrapped parcels, two magazines, a book and a capacious handbag. Peter watched in amusement as she tried to hold on to all these articles and at the same time open her bag to pay the taxi. One of the parcels fell to the ground and the taxi-driver stooped to pick it up.

'Here you are, Peter,' Claude said from behind him.

Peter turned apologetically and took the suitcase from Claude.

'Thanks. Well, it's been great seeing you, Claude. I'll try and find an excuse to come out to Stockholm when you're playing there.'

'Please do. I get so tired of always being among strangers. You've no idea what a difference it makes to know you're in the audience.'

'*Attention, s'il vous plait*,' the porter called out from behind them. The overburdened woman had managed to pay off the taxi-driver.

Claude and Peter moved to make way for the little procession. As the porter and his customer went past the largest of the parcels escaped from under her arm and fell to the ground. She stooped to pick it up and as she did so one of the magazines slipped from her grasp.

Peter exchanged a smile with Claude and went to her rescue. He picked up the parcel and magazine, put the former in her hands and tucked the latter under her arm.

'Oh, thank you,' she said breathlessly, reinforcing his impression that despite the continental style of dress she was English.

'Not at all.' Peter was still watching her as she turned to follow the porter.

'I won't come any further,' Claude said. 'I think this policeman has his eye on me.'

Peter was in ample time for his flight. After checking in his baggage he wandered round the shopping arcade, idly looking for anything that might do as a present for his secretary. He decided on a box of Swiss chocolates and drifted on to the bookstall to select something light to read on the flight.

She was standing at the cashier's desk, trying to pay for a paperback novel she had bought. She had got rid of her two suitcases but had evidently been reluctant to part with her parcels. As Peter came up behind her to pay for his copy of *Punch* another parcel tumbled to the ground. This time it was a small one with gilt paper secured by a silver ribbon tied in an elaborate bow. Peter picked it up and waited till she had received her change. Then she turned, with a smile ready for her rescuer.

'Oh!' The smile widened when she saw Peter.

'Yes, I'm afraid it's me again.'

As she still did not have a hand free he balanced the small parcel on top of the big one. She clutched it against her chest.

'Thank you very much!' she said, laughingly.

Peter nodded and smiled back at her. She moved away while he searched his pockets for all the small change he could get rid of before boarding.

He saw her again when he passed through Emigration into the main departure lounge. She had looked wistfully into the Duty-Free shop and reluctantly decided that she could not carry any more. Peter availed himself of the opportunity to buy his allowance of spirits and cigarettes, so he was himself well loaded as he boarded the aircraft.

He believed he was entitled to his creature comforts when he went abroad on behalf of the firm and more often than not travelled first class. Mollie Stafford had booked him a window seat for both the outward and inward flights. As he gently but firmly pushed his way towards the seat which the air hostess had indicated, someone jogged his arm. His copy of *Punch* slipped from under his arm and fell to the floor. He was jammed in by other passengers and it was a moment or two before he was able to gain sufficient elbow room to retrieve it. As he turned round a passenger picked up the magazine and quietly handed it to him. Before he had time to say anything the girl burst out laughing. Her laughter was infectious and, to the astonishment of the harassed people behind him, Peter started laughing too.

The first class compartment was not fully booked and the seat next to Peter was empty. A few minutes later the girl with the auburn hair was settling into the seat next to him. As she strapped herself in and waited for the take-off she was silent and a little aloof. But when the aircraft levelled out and the hostess came round with drinks, she loosened the seat belt and tilted her seat back with a sigh of relief.

'Thank you.' She took the glass from the hostess and smiled at Peter. 'I can do with this.'

Then he understood the reason for her silence and tension.

'Are you nervous of flying?'

'No. Just petrified. Especially at take-off and landing.'

'I don't think anyone likes that part.'

Beyond the window the Lake of Geneva suddenly vanished as the aircraft passed through a thick cloud. Peter opened a packet of his duty-free cigarettes. He offered his companion one. She shook her head, and watched him as he lit his own.

'Excuse my asking,' she said after a moment. 'But— that man who was seeing you off at the airport. Was it Claude Matty, the pianist?'

'Yes,' Peter said with a certain pride. 'It was.'

'I thought so! He's not someone you could easily mistake.'

'He was giving a recital last night in Geneva.'

'Yes, I know. I went to it.'

Peter looked at her with a new interest. 'Did you enjoy it?'

'Very much,' she said enthusiastically. 'I think he's fabulous. The first time I heard him play was in Washington about seven years ago. I thought then he was fabulous and I still think so. Is he a friend of yours?'

'He's my brother.'

She appeared to be taken aback by this statement, as if she had been saying something derogatory about Claude. 'Oh!' she said, at a loss for words. 'Oh, really?'

'Really,' Peter repeated, smiling at her embarrassment.

'Well, I think he's absolutely—'

'Fabulous?'

She laughed and nodded. 'Yes.'

'I'll tell him so.'

'I'm sure he's used to people telling him how wonderful he is.'

'Yes, but he still likes to hear it.'

She finished her champagne, lowered the table fixed to the back of the seat in front of her and put the glass down on it.

'Are you a musician, Mr—Matty?'

'Peter Matty. No, I'm a publisher of books.' He nodded at the paperback lying on her lap, the one she had bought in the airport shop. 'As a matter of fact, that's one of ours.'

'Oh!' She picked the book up and studied the jacket illustration critically.

'I gather you don't like the jacket.'

'Not very much.' She put the book down again. 'Do you go to many of your brother's concerts?'

'Not as many as I'd like to.'

'I imagine he travels a great deal.'

'Yes, a great deal. All over the world in fact. Are you on holiday, Miss—er?'

'Mrs,' she said, spreading her left hand to display the wedding ring on her finger. 'My name is du Salle. Phyllis du Salle.'

'Mrs du Salle.' It was quite unreasonable but Peter felt a little pang of disappointment.

'Yes.' She was looking at him with a faintly amused smile, as if she had guessed his thoughts. 'I suppose you could call it a holiday. This is my first visit to England, although, curiously enough, my husband was English. He emigrated to America in 1970.'

Peter noted that she spoke of her husband in the past tense, but he made no comment.

She paused for a moment before adding, very quietly, 'Norman, my husband, was killed in an accident about six months ago.'

'Oh, I am sorry.' As always on such occasions there was an awkward silence. To break it Peter asked: 'And you've never been to England?'

'No, I haven't. Norman and I used to talk about it. We made plans on more than one occasion but somehow they never worked out.'

Peter noticed that she spoke of her husband and used his name without emotion.

'But—forgive me. Your accent.'

'It's very English?' she said, raising one eyebrow.

'Yes,' Peter said bluntly.

She laughed. 'I know. Everyone tells me that. Actually I

19

was born in Boston. My father was in the State Department and we were constantly meeting English people, so probably that has something to do with it.'

The hostess came round with a fresh bottle of champagne. They both held out their glasses for a refill.

'Where are you staying in England?' Peter asked casually.

'I shall be in London for four or five days and then I'm probably going down to Dorset.'

The suggestion of an American accent had come through in her pronunciation of that last word. She corrected herself, with exaggerated Englishness. 'Dawset. Is that right?'

'Yes,' Peter agreed, smiling as he saw her eyebrow go up again. 'That's right.'

'A great friend of my late husband lives at a place called Heatherdown.'

'Oh, I know Heatherdown.'

'You do?'

'Yes, quite well. I have a boat at Poole Harbour. It's about twelve miles away. You'll like Heatherdown. It's a very nice little town.'

'So I'm told. Perhaps you know Sir Arnold Wyatt?'

'No, I don't think so. I can't recall that name.'

'He's a barrister. At least he was. I believe he retired a couple of years ago.'

She opened her handbag and found a small Morocco leather diary. She leafed through the pages to the Addresses section. 'Forest Gate Manor, Orchard Place, Heatherdown.'

She glanced enquiringly at Peter. He shook his head. She put the diary back in her handbag and snapped it shut.

'We've never met but I feel as if we're old friends.' She paused and then added in more reverential tones, 'My husband's parents died when he was quite young and Sir Arnold looked after him for a while. Norman was very fond of him.'

'Was your husband a lawyer?'

'No, he was a journalist. He was quite well known in America.'

'Norman du Salle.' The name had now awakened a chord in Peter's memory. 'Yes, of course.'

'You probably read about the accident. It was in all the papers.'

Peter studied her with renewed interest, trying to recall the details of the reports he had read six months ago. He was about to question her further, then changed his mind. The aircraft had come through the cloud stratum. They were in blazing sunshine and a landscape of white cotton wool lay below them. It was dazzling to the eyes. He stubbed his cigarette out in the ash-tray recessed into the side of his seat, took out his wallet and extracted one of his business cards.

'If I can help you at all while you are in London, please don't hesitate to give me a ring.'

'That's more than kind of you, Mr Matty. I appreciate it.' She took the card. Her head tilted to one side as she read the address, then she gave him her smile. 'I shall be staying at the Connaught Hotel.'

3

For the first couple of days after his return from Geneva Peter was extremely busy. Things had piled up during his absence and he had to give priority to a number of urgent matters. As some of them concerned the foreign rights of books he had to do a lot of telephoning out of normal London office hours. On one occasion during those hectic forty-eight hours his taxi actually passed the Connaught and for a moment he thought of calling in there on the off-chance of seeing Phyllis du Salle. But he was already late and the taxi had passed before he could make up his mind.

It was not till Wednesday, two days after his return, that he had time to see Max Lerner. Even then he could only fit him in by taking him out to lunch, so that they could discuss business over the meal. When his receptionist announced the visitor Peter came down to meet him in the entrance hall of the building.

Max was a young Fleet Street journalist whom Peter used when he wanted elusive facts and figures dug up. He had an uncanny knack for ferreting out the truth and seemed to know instinctively where to look for his material. He had just completed a particularly tricky piece of research for Matty Books Ltd. He was an irrepressibly cheerful character, small in stature but full of bounce and confidence. He had curly hair and a chubby, smiling face. Though as ugly as a gargoyle he was remarkably successful with women, a success which had led to the break-up of three marriages already. His eyes were continually on the move, usually following the nearest attractive girl. He smoked a special brand of long, thin cigars.

'You've got your report there, Max?' Peter inquired, when he'd greeted his friend with a slap on the shoulder. Max tapped the briefcase he had under his arm. 'Then we'll go straight on to the restaurant. Mollie telephoned for a taxi. It should be here any minute.'

The taxi drew up as they emerged from the front door. Peter gave directions to the driver and soon they were in the thick traffic moving along the Euston Road.

'It's been a pretty hard slog, Peter, I can tell you,' Max was saying. 'Far more difficult than I expected.'

Peter was accustomed to this kind of softening-up from Max. 'Yes, I know. And I know the next line too, Max. You're being grossly underpaid.'

'Well, you're the one who's said it!' Max gave his throaty laugh and lit up another of his cigars. 'Tell me, how did you get on in Geneva?'

'It was a wonderful evening. I must say they gave Claude a marvellous reception. He was delighted—as he had every reason to be.'

'How is your brother?'

'He's fine. Working far too hard as usual. Have you met Claude?'

'Yes. I met him several years ago. I interviewed him for some magazine. I doubt very much whether he'd remember me. God, this London traffic gets worse every day!'

The taxi driver was trying to swap lanes so that he could sneak through on the left hand side. He was blocked by a red Metro, whose driver refused to yield to the taxi. The taxi driver muttered something uncomplimentary about female drivers. Max was gazing with interest at the object of his remarks. Peter followed his eyes and his heart gave a jump. The driver of the Metro was Phyllis du Salle. She was staring straight ahead, her eyes on the traffic lights, apparently oblivious that she was the focus for three men.

Max's mouth dropped as Peter leant forward and opened the window. He put his head out and shouted: 'Dropped any good parcels lately?'

Phyllis turned her head. Her expression was frosty as she prepared to give her accoster the brush-off. It changed when she recognised Peter. She smiled broadly.

'Why, hello!'

'How do you like London?'

'I think it's absolutely—'

'Fabulous?'

Phyllis laughed. 'That's right.'

Ahead the traffic light had turned green. The cars ahead started to move forward.

'What are you doing tonight?'

'I don't know. I haven't thought about it.'

'Let's have dinner. I'll pick you up at eight o'clock.'

The taxi driver was not to be outdone. Forcing his way in ahead of Phyllis he forced her to brake. As the taxi moved ahead Peter stuck his head out even further and shouted back: 'Eight o'clock!'

She gave him a wave and a nod. As he closed the window and sat back in his seat Max was contemplating him with admiration.

'You bachelors certainly know how to take advantage of the traffic.'

'Her name's Phyllis du Salle. I met her on the plane coming back from Geneva.'

'du Salle?'

'Yes.'

24

'Any relation to Norman du Salle?'

'His wife,' Peter said, surprised at Max's perspicacity. 'Widow, I should say. Did you know Norman du Salle?'

'No, not really. I met him once at a press conference. He was a sort of political gossip writer. No, I suppose that's a little unkind because he made quite a name for himself.' Max leant forward to tap the ash from his cigarillo into an ash tray. 'The poor devil was drowned, you know.'

'What happened exactly?'

'I was in Paris at the time of the accident. The French papers were full of it. If I remember rightly Mrs du Salle and her husband were on a trip to Europe. They decided to visit Corsica and boarded a ship at Marseilles. Apparently they had a very rough passage. Heavy seas—the lot. The guy just disappeared.'

'What do you mean—disappeared?'

'He apparently fell overboard.'

'Good God!'

Peter had to put a hand onto the seat to steady himself as the driver took a sharp left-hand turn.

'His body was washed up several days later and—Phyllis, did you say her name was?'

'Yes.'

'Phyllis identified it.'

'Poor girl!' Peter spoke with such genuine feeling that Max looked at him curiously. 'What a terrible experience!'

'Yes, it was. In more ways than one.' Max's tone was sceptical, as if he was implying that Peter's sympathy might be misplaced. 'There was a lot of gossip. Talk of suicide. Several of the papers inferred that there had been a quarrel of some kind.'

'Had there been a quarrel?' Peter asked.

'Yes, I'm afraid so. His wife admitted it at the inquest.

Fortunately for her they brought in a verdict of accidental death. Personally I don't think the row had anything to do with him going overboard. You don't commit suicide over a doll.'

'A doll?'

'Yes. If I remember rightly the quarrel was some petty disagreement over a doll.'

Peter might have asked Max some more questions about the affair but at that moment the taxi driver did a sudden U-turn and stopped outside the Greek restaurant where he'd booked a table. During lunch their conversation concentrated on the research work Max had done and they did not return to the subject of Phyllis du Salle.

On his way back from lunch Peter called in on a printer who was quoting very competitive rates, so it was after four o'clock when he returned to his office. His thoughts as he went upstairs to the first floor were that his date with Phyllis was less than four hours away.

He could hear the sound of Mollie's electric typewriter as he opened the door of her office.

'Hello, Mollie!'

She glanced up, surprised at the cheerfulness in his voice. 'That call came through from New York. They're ringing again at five o'clock—our time.'

'Bully for New York!'

Mollie looked at him more closely. Peter was usually careful about how much he drank at lunch but today he sounded quite high.

'The Lazenby contract's arrived. I put it on your desk.'

'Splendid!' Peter responded in the same euphoric tone.

His step was springy as he crossed to the door of his own office. He had his fingers on the door handle when she stopped him dead in his tracks.

'Oh—and a Mrs du Salle phoned.'

'Yes?' Peter said without turning.

'She says she's very sorry but she can't see you this evening after all.'

Peter spun round. The on-top-of-the-world expression had vanished. 'She can't see me?'

'That's right.'

'Is that all she said?'

'Yes,' Mollie told him firmly, 'that's all.'

'Did she ask to speak to me?'

'No. She just left the message.'

He stared at her for five seconds as if he doubted whether she was telling the truth, then slowly let out his breath.

'I see. Thank you, Mollie.'

He went into his office, closing the door gently. She went on looking at the door after he had disappeared. She knew that she had passed on the message with unnecessary terseness, but she could not help feeling a certain satisfaction at having so thoroughly deflated him.

It took Peter twice as long as usual to check through the Lazenby contract. He found it equally hard to concentrate on the readers' reports on a number of manuscripts which had been submitted. Phyllis had seemed genuinely glad to see him in that traffic jam. He was at a complete loss to account for her cancelling the date in such an impersonal way. He was on the point of telephoning her several times to ask her point blank what it was all about but each time he stopped himself. He stayed on in the office for an hour and a half after Mollie had left, trying to make up for the time he had lost. When at last he left the building he had decided what he was going to do.

He was lucky to pick up a cruising taxi in Russell Square.

The driver heard his shout and pulled in to the kerb beside him.

'Connaught Hotel,' Peter directed him.

It was a little before half past seven when his taxi driver set him down near the front entrance to the hotel. He was paying him off when he became aware that a couple of women had come out through the doors. When he turned round he saw that one of them was Phyllis du Salle. She had her back to him and was obviously saying goodbye to her companion. The latter was slightly older, and had made too obvious use of lipstick and eye-shadow to mask that fact. Her clothes were good but a little too extravagant in style. She was obviously observant, especially where men were concerned, and had registered Peter as soon as he started walking towards the hotel entrance. As he came nearer he could hear from her voice that she was American.

'I'll pick you up tomorrow morning, honey,' she was saying, 'at about eleven.'

'Yes, all right, Linda,' Phyllis said. She was still unaware of Peter's presence.

'Are you sure you won't have dinner with me this evening?'

'Absolutely sure.' Phyllis shook her head apologetically. 'It's very kind of you and I appreciate it but I really must have an early night for a change. Truly, darling.'

The other woman was now watching Peter with un-disguised interest. He had stopped a few yards behind Phyllis.

'All right, my dear, if that's what you want.' She bent forward and gave Phyllis a peck on the cheek. 'Take care of yourself.'

Peter realised that he could not just stand there listening

28

any longer. He took another step forward and said, 'Good evening.'

Phyllis turned in surprise. When she saw Peter she was nonplussed for a moment. 'Oh! Hello!' she said, obviously embarrassed. 'Didn't you get my message?'

'Yes, I did,' Peter said calmly. 'Thank you very much.'

He gave Linda a smile. Immensely intrigued by what she had guessed was a potentially romantic situation she returned his smile with interest. After an awkward silence Phyllis realised that she had no alternative but to introduce them.

'This is a friend of mine. Mrs Braithwaite. Mr—Matty.'

Linda offered her hand for Peter to shake. As he took it he could feel the large rings on her fingers.

'Mr Matty,' she said, putting so much warmth into the mere repetition of his name that it sounded like a verbal caress.

'Pleased to meet you, Mrs Braithwaite.'

'Well, I guess I'll be making a move,' Linda said with heavy tactfulness. She included them both in a conspiratorial smile. 'It was a lovely surprise bumping into you, Phyllis. I'm looking forward to tomorrow morning.'

'Me too, Linda.'

'Goodbye, Mr Matty. So nice to have met you.'

'Goodbye, Mrs Braithwaite,' Peter said, trying not to make it sound too obvious that he wished she would take herself off.

Linda gave Phyllis a little wave of her hand and set off towards Berkeley Square. Phyllis turned to face Peter.

'I met Linda in Switzerland,' she explained awkwardly. 'We became quite friendly. I'd no idea she was in London.'

'Oh,' Peter said, nodding seriously, 'I see.'

'I'm sorry about tonight,' she hurried on, 'but I've had a frightfully busy day, and—'

'Not to worry. That's all right.'

'I really had a hectic time,' she insisted, 'and I thought I'd like to—have an early night for a change.'

'Why not?' Peter said in that same equable tone. To prevent her breaking off and retreating into the hotel he asked, 'How do you like the Metro?'

'The Metro? Oh, the car! Very much. I love driving it.'

'Even in London?'

'Yes, even in London.'

'My word, you are a glutton for punishment.'

He had kept a straight face and she was not sure whether he was paying her a compliment or making fun of her.

'I rented it. The car, I mean.'

'Yes. Yes, I rather thought you had.'

She gave him a puzzled look in which there was a slight resentment at being caught in such an embarrassing situation. 'Well—good night, Mr Matty.'

Peter glanced at his watch. 'Half past seven. You are having an early night! Look, if we can't have dinner together won't you let me buy you a drink?' Seeing her hesitate he added quickly, 'A very small drink. You can drink it very quickly.'

Suddenly she smiled and nodded. 'A small, quick drink, but it's still no to dinner, I'm afraid.'

They had their drink in the oak-panelled cocktail bar of the Connaught. Peter ordered a dry martini and Phyllis a scotch with Malvern water. She was friendly and pleasant but without showing any warmth. He felt that she was keeping him at a distance. It was only after he had persuaded her to accept a second drink that she began to talk about her husband. He had asked her when she was going down to Heatherdown.

'At the weekend. I spoke to Sir Arnold this morning. I believe I told you about Sir Arnold Wyatt.'

'Yes, you did.'

'He sounded awfully nice on the phone, which was quite a relief.'

'Why a relief?'

'Well, over the years I had heard so much about him from my husband. I suddenly felt nervous of meeting him. I don't quite know why. Up till now I've been looking forward to it. Anyway, I'm sure he's very nice.'

She smiled, and accepted an olive from the dish he pushed towards her.

'Yes, I'm sure he is. Will you be staying in Heatherdown?'

'I think so. Sir Arnold invited me down for the weekend, but to be truthful I haven't decided whether I shall stay with him or not.' She put the olive in her mouth, biting on it carefully to make sure there was no stone in it. He waited, half hoping that she would ask if he had room for a visitor on his boat. Instead she asked him a quite unexpected question. 'This morning, when you passed me in the taxi, you had a friend with you.'

'Yes. Max Lerner. He's a journalist.'

'Max Lerner!' She nodded, pleased with herself. 'That's right! I thought I recognised him. I couldn't remember his name.'

'You know Max?' Peter said with surprise.

'We've met. A long time ago. I was with my husband. He probably doesn't remember.'

'No,' he said dryly. 'I don't think he does.'

She leant forward. 'What did Mr Lerner tell you?'

'Tell me? About what?'

'About my husband. About the accident.'

'Oh, he just said he was in Paris when it happened and he'd read about it.'

'In the French newspapers?'

'Yes.'

Her expression had become serious. There was a shaded light on the wall behind her and leaning forward had brought her face into shadow.

'Did he tell you about the quarrel I had with my husband?'

Peter hesitated to answer, not wanting to re-open old wounds for her. 'Yes, I think so,' he said vaguely. 'I believe he mentioned it.'

'It was a stupid, ridiculous row,' she said angrily. 'It ought never to have happened. It was about a doll that Norman bought just before we left Marseilles.'

He recalled Max's scathing comment about two adults quarrelling over a doll. He waited, sensing that for some reason she wanted to tell him about it.

'I know it sounds odd but my husband was crazy about dolls. He just couldn't resist them—especially if they wore national costumes. German dolls, Swiss dolls, French dolls. You name them, he bought them!'

Peter could not help smiling at her vehemence. 'Well, people do collect all sorts of things. Believe it or not I have a friend who collects shoe-horns. He's got over two hundred of them.'

'Shoe-horns? That's unusual.'

'Yes, it is. He still uses his fingers when he puts his shoes on.'

The smile which so beguiled him suddenly lit up her face. She saw his expression and gazed back at him steadily for a moment.

'You were telling me about your husband,' he prompted.

She watched a man and woman come in and seat them-selves at a nearby table. He was wondering whether she was going to ignore the hint when she began to speak in a voice so low that he had to lean forward to catch what she said.

'We'd purchased a Land-Rover in Paris and were taking it from Marseilles to Corsica on the overnight boat. It was a dark, unpleasant night and when we left Marseilles there was quite obviously a storm blowing up. We'd been at sea for about an hour and I was searching for some sea-sick tablets when I realised that I had forgotten to pack Norman's doll. I told him and he was extremely annoyed—to put it mildly.'

She was not looking at him but staring at the far wall of the room, seeing past it to that night on the storm-tossed ship.

'Well, one thing led to another and he finally lost his temper with me. He banged out of the cabin and went up on deck. I stayed in the cabin for a while and then decided that I'd better go after him. I couldn't find him anywhere! He wasn't on deck or in any of the public rooms. I searched the entire boat. I looked everywhere but I just couldn't find him. In the end, of course, I had to send for the Captain.'

Though she was speaking in a flat voice he knew that recalling the incident must be causing her a lot of distress. He felt compunction for having led her on, but in a way it was a compliment that she had felt like unburdening herself to him.

'The next day, as you can imagine, I was utterly and completely bewildered. I just did not know what on earth to do. In the end I flew back to Marseilles.'

'It must have been terrible for you,' he said, with genuine concern.

'It was. And the papers didn't exactly help, I'm afraid.'

He realised that the smoke from his cigarette was drifting towards her face and waved his hand to disperse it. 'Did you—did you ever find the doll?'

'After the accident I forgot all about it. It went completely out of my mind. Then one night—' The far-away expression had come back, but now she was looking at Peter. Her eyes were unfocussed and she seemed to be seeing straight through him. 'One night I was staying at a small hotel just off La Canebière.'

'In Marseilles?'

'Yes. I went out for a walk. When I came back I went into the bathroom and—there it was!'

'The doll?'

She nodded. 'While I had been out someone had filled the bath and the doll was floating on top of the water.'

'The same doll?' Peter asked incredulously.

'I think it was the same doll. It certainly looked exactly like it. About an hour later the police telephoned me. I was asked to come and identify my husband's body. It had been washed up on some beach.'

'Why, that's an incredible story!' Peter had forgotten his cigarette. His hand jerked as it burned his fingers. He quickly stubbed it out.

'Did you tell the police what had happened? I mean, about the doll?'

'Yes, I did. They simply took possession of it and said nothing. Whether the doll was important or not I don't know. They didn't tell me and I did not feel like asking them. I just wanted to leave Marseilles and get back to America. To get home.'

'My God, yes! I can well understand that.'

She leant back, saw that there was still a little whisky left in her glass. She drank it, put the glass down and stood up.

'Well, that's it, Mr Matty. Now you know the whole story.' She put her hand out and he automatically shook it. 'Thank you for the drink.'

Before he could think of an excuse to stop her going, she had walked across the cocktail bar. He stared after her till she had disappeared through the door. She did not look back.

4

Peter's first act on reaching his office next morning was to telephone Phyllis du Salle. He had slept badly, lying awake for long periods in the darkness thinking about her and the extraordinary story she had told him. The fact that she had felt like confiding in him about those tragic events must surely mean that she regarded him as more than just a casual acquaintance. She had probably left him so abruptly because she did not want to give way to her emotion in his presence. Long before daylight came round the edge of his bedroom curtains he knew that he had to see her again.

The operator at the Connaught put his call through to Phyllis's room. She sounded genuinely glad to hear his voice and he was emboldened to propose the plan he had dreamt up while he was having breakfast.

'I'm going down to do some work on my boat over the weekend. Poole is only about twelve miles from Heatherdown, so why don't you let me drive you down there?'

He half-expected her to turn down the suggestion but to his surprise she seemed grateful and immediately accepted. He arranged to pick her up at her hotel on the Friday after an early lunch.

On the arranged day he managed to get away from the office in good time. He collected his car and drove round to the Connaught. There were no traffic wardens about so he parked the Jaguar XJS on a yellow line opposite the hotel and walked across Carlos Place. Linda Braithwaite was just coming out of the hotel. She was heading for the taxi which the commissionaire had hailed for her when she spotted Peter.

'Hello, Mr Matty!' she called gaily. 'Phyllis is ready. She'll be with you in a moment.'

She waited till he had come up alongside her. She was wearing a completely different outfit from the last time he had seen her. This time the theme was Cambridge blue, even down to the shoes and handbag. 'I've just been saying goodbye to her,' she beamed. 'I'm flying back to the States this evening. And very sorry to be leaving, I might add.'

'You'll have to pay us another visit,' he said gallantly.

'I certainly will!' she agreed with great emphasis. 'I'm crazy about London. But who isn't?'

The taxi driver had not moved from his seat. Peter opened the door for her. She climbed in and sat down. Before he shut the door she leant forward, the same conspiratorial smile on her face. 'Have a lovely weekend— and take care of Phyllis.'

He nodded and closed the door. As the taxi pulled away Phyllis came out of the hotel followed by one of the Connaught's porters carrying her suitcase. She waved at the departing Linda, whose hand could be seen fluttering behind the rear window.

'Sorry if I'm late.'

'I've only just arrived. You've had lunch?'

'Oh, I'm not worried about lunch.' She glanced up at the sky, where white clouds were drifting slowly across the blue. 'Is it going to keep fine?'

'I think so.'

She was dressed for the country in well-cut green velvet

slacks. The matching jacket was draped over her shoulders, the sleeves hanging loose. She had tied a scarlet ribbon round her hair, which had the effect of making her look even younger.

'The car's across the road,' Peter told the porter and led the way through the traffic.

He opened the boot of the white sports Jaguar so that the porter could put the suitcase in it. It was already nearly full of gear which he was taking down to the boat. Phyllis was admiring the low, sleek lines of the car with their unmistakable suggestion of power and speed.

'My goodness, what a lovely car!'

Peter secured the boot and tipped the porter. He walked round the car and handed her the keys.

'It's all yours.'

'What do you mean?'

'You said you were crazy about driving.'

'I am.'

'Well, I hate it. So you go ahead and drive.'

'Why do people who hate driving always have the nicest cars?' She was looking at the keys, a little wary of handling such an exotic vehicle but obviously tempted. 'Are you serious?'

'Absolutely.'

'What happens if I smash into something?'

'I shall bail out.'

She was a good driver and it was soon obvious that in the States she'd had plenty of experience with cars much bigger than the Jaguar. They were early enough to beat the Friday afternoon rush to leave London. By the time they had passed Richmond and Twickenham she had the feel of the car. After Sunbury, where they came onto the M3, she put her foot down and the car's speed rose to a hundred miles an hour. Her driving was so sure and confident that Peter's only qualms were for lurking police cars and radar traps.

It was not yet three as they sped along the M27 to the north of Southampton. Well before half past the Jaguar slid through the narrow streets of Poole's Old Town. Peter directed Phyllis alongside the port to the place where he kept his boat. It lay in a small harbour to the south of the main quay. The little anchorage was used principally by fishing boats and was protected by a low breakwater. The great advantage of this mooring was that he could park his car close alongside.

She switched the engine off and looked round at him with a smile.

'You didn't have to bail out.'

'I enjoyed every minute of it,' he said with sincerity.

Peter's boat was an eight-metre cruiser-racer of 6.3 tons. She had the clean lines and soaring mast of a sailing yacht, but she was also equipped with an auxiliary engine so that she could travel under her own power. The local fisherman who looked after her for him had made her ready for his visit. He helped Phyllis down the steps in the harbour wall and handed her across the little companionway onto the deck.

She stood for a minute gazing across the water at the pine-green hump of Brownsea Island, the breeze from the sea stirring her hair. Then her eyes came back to the yacht with its sparkling white paintwork, polished mahogany and gleaming brass.

'Do you like it?'

'Yes, I do.' She was looking at the name stencilled on a life-belt hanging by the entrance to the cabin. '*First Edition*. Is that its name?'

'Yes. Frightfully original. One of our authors suggested it should be called *Out of Print*.'

They both laughed. They were standing very close together on the deck aft of the cabin. The sun was reflected warmly onto their faces from the water of the harbour.

'What time did you say you'd get to Heatherdown?'

'I said about half past three or four.'

Peter glanced at his watch. 'That's fine. I'll just put my things on board and then we'll drive over there.'

She put a hand on his arm. 'Peter, there's no need for you to come. Really. I can surely pick up a cab—'

'Nonsense! If you think I'm going to let you—' He stopped, obviously struck by an idea. 'Wait a minute! I'll tell you what you can do. You can borrow the car.'

'No, really. I couldn't do that.'

'Why not? It's a splendid idea. That way I'm bound to see you again because you'll have to bring it back.'

She was about to protest again when he put his hand out and placed his index finger on her lips. 'No, seriously. It's a very sensible suggestion. Suppose you don't like this Sir Arnold character?'

'I'm sure I will.'

'But just supposing you don't. Then all you've got to do is tell him about your friends in Bournemouth, jump in the car and come back here.'

'What friends in Bournemouth?'

'Such old, old friends,' he said with mock seriousness. 'They'd be very upset if you decided to stay anywhere else.'

She was looking at him steadily, a flicker of a smile at the corners of her mouth. 'You sound very experienced at this sort of thing, Mr Matty.'

'Oh, but I am. I've got girlfriends all over the place. When I've got my gear on board I'll take you round the corner and introduce you to one of them.'

'Mrs Frinton, I'd like to introduce you to a friend of mine. This is Mrs du Salle.'

'Pleased to meet you.' Mrs Frinton's round, jolly face creased into a smile of welcome. She reached across the counter to shake Phyllis's hand. She was in her early sixties, with white hair above pink cheeks and a pair of startlingly modern spectacles. Phyllis exchanged a secret smile with Peter.

Mrs Frinton's little shop was in the maze of narrow streets at the back of the harbour. She sold newspapers and magazines, sweets and cigarettes. She was also a sub-postmistress and dispensed stamps and retirement pensions from behind a little grille at one side of the shop. A public coin-box telephone was fixed to one wall.

'Down here for a holiday, Mr Matty?' she asked.

'That's right. I've got one or two jobs to do on the boat.'

'You've got some nice weather for it.'

Mrs Frinton pretended to rearrange the newspapers laid out on the counter, but she was really giving Phyllis a close inspection round the side of her glasses.

'Makes a change, doesn't it? Mrs Frinton, Mrs du Salle is going over to Heatherdown to visit some friends of hers, and I've arranged for her to telephone you this evening and leave a message for me. Is that convenient?'

'Yes, of course, dearie.' Mrs Frinton smiled reassuringly at Phyllis. 'No problem. Shall I write the number down for you?'

Phyllis was obviously delighted by the tiny shop and its homely postmistress. She was smiling as Mrs Frinton

41

wrote a number down on one of her sweet bags and handed it to her.

'Thank you, Mrs Frinton. Poole 895674.'

'That's right, my dear. Don't worry. I'll see he gets the message.'

'It'll probably be about six o'clock when I phone,' Phyllis said, putting the folded paper in her handbag.

'I'll be here, dearie.' The postmistress gave Peter a nod. 'I'll pop up to the boat with the message.'

When Phyllis had driven off, carefully primed by Peter on how to find the road to Heatherdown, he went back on board his boat and began to sort out the gear he had brought from the car and dumped on the deck. There were several jobs he wanted to get done in preparation for Phyllis's possible return. The time passed quickly. At ten past six, when Mrs Frinton had not shown up, he decided to walk round to the shop. He caught her in the act of locking the door and hanging up the CLOSED sign.

'No.' she told him. 'There's been no message. But don't worry, Mr Matty, if the phone rings I'll hear it and as soon as the young lady telephones I'll let you know.'

'Are you going out this evening, Mrs Frinton?'

'No, I'm not.' She laughed at the concern on his face. 'I'll be watching telly.'

When he was alone Peter often had his evening meal in one of the Poole restaurants but that night he stayed on board to wait for the message. He cooked himself a late meal and afterwards sat on the deck with a drink, watching the sun set over the low Dorset hills to the west. By eleven o'clock he was forced to the conclusion that Sir Arnold Wyatt had prevailed on her to stay at Forest Gate Manor. He could not help feeling disappointed, and a little hurt that she had not even bothered to telephone.

He did not manage to get to sleep until the small hours and as a consequence did not wake up until nine o'clock. After he had breakfasted and made the boat ship-shape he wandered up to Mrs Frinton's shop. She had already been open for an hour and a half and was taking advantage of a lull to do her accounts.

'Good morning, Mr Matty. No message yet, I'm afraid.'

'I see. May I have a look at your local telephone directory?'

He had made up his mind that if there was no message he would telephone Sir Arnold Wyatt's house. He took the directory she handed him to a shelf under the window overlooking the street. As he was leafing through it he heard the sound of a car echoing between the houses. He looked up and saw a white Jaguar XJS flash past. He dashed out of the shop in time to see it turn onto the quayside. He was smiling with pleasure and relief as he broke into a run to follow it.

When he came into view of his boat he saw that the white Jaguar was already parked beside it. As he came abreast of it, breathless from running, he saw that there was no one in it. He moved to the edge of the quay. There was no sign of anyone on the yacht either. He stood there, looking to right and left for any sign of Phyllis. It seemed impossible that she could have disappeared so quickly.

A voice behind him said: 'Good morning.'

He spun round. A young policeman in a peaked cap was just emerging from the cabin.

'Good morning,' he answered warily.

'Are you the owner of this boat, sir?'

'Yes, I am.'

'Then you're Mr Matty. And I take it that's your car?'

'Yes. Look, what's happened? What's this all about?'

The policeman did not answer, but came across the little companionway onto the quay. As he did so Peter heard another car come up fast. It was a police car painted in the livery of the county traffic police. It halted beside the Jaguar.

'Was your car stolen, sir?' the young officer said behind him.

'No. Of course it wasn't! If it had been stolen I'd have reported it. I lent it to a friend of mine.'

Peter was beginning to become irritated by the air of mystery which the police officer seemed determined to create.

'Look, would you please tell me what you're doing with my car?'

The policeman, inured to members of the public who became over-excited when questioned, calmly produced a piece of paper from his pocket. Without comment he handed it to Peter.

He unfolded it and read: 'Please return this car to Mr Peter Matty, c/o Yacht "First Edition", Poole Harbour.'

He looked up into the expressionless eyes of the policeman, who nodded towards the Jaguar.

'We found that on the windscreen. The car was abandoned in a private lane leading to a farm at Landon Cross.'

'Landon Cross?' The name meant nothing to Peter.

'About a mile and a half from Heatherdown.' The policeman was contemplating Peter thoughtfully, perhaps making up his mind that he was not a potential criminal so much as a gullible fool. 'You say you lent your car to a friend?'

'That's right. She was visiting someone in Heatherdown.'

The young man gave him a more understanding look, implying that the 'she' explained many things.

'Yes. Well, it's a very nice car, sir. I'd be careful who I lent it to in future. Incidentally your friend went off with the key. We had a devil of a job finding one to fit. Have you got a spare?'

'Yes, I have.'

'Well, you might as well have this one. It's no longer any use to us.'

Peter took the key absent-mindedly. 'Thank you.' Then he pulled himself together and said more warmly: 'And thank you for returning the car, officer.'

'It was a pleasure driving it.' Now that the job was over the young policeman relaxed, even going so far as to smile. 'Wish it was mine.'

He gave Peter a friendly nod and ran to join his two colleagues in the waiting patrol car. As it drove off the occupants stared at Peter, sharing some joke amongst themselves.

Heatherdown was a pleasant Dorset market town. Its long main street was flanked by a number of half-timbered houses. The hostelry in the small square was genuine Tudor. Though it lay several miles from the sea, the river which ran past the edge of the town was navigable for small craft. There were a number of yachts and cabin cruisers moored by the bridge carrying the road to Corfe.

Peter drove slowly along the street looking for someone intelligent of whom he could ask directions. There were a number of obvious holidaymakers about, recognisable by their jeans, gaudy shirts and general air of aimlessness. He decided he would do better to ask at a shop and drew up

45

opposite a photographer's in whose window a number of groups and portraits were displayed.

As he opened the car door he almost bumped into a middle-aged woman who was pushing a shopping trolley along the pavement. They both apologised.

'Excuse me,' Peter said. 'But can you direct me to Forest Gate Manor?'

'Forest Gate Manor,' she repeated in her Dorset accent, looking at him with interest and respect. The name was evidently familiar to her. 'You go down to the bridge. You see, there in front of you? Turn right along the quayside. Past the boat shed you'll see the entrance to the Manor. You can't miss it.'

He followed her directions and presently was passing through the open gates at the bottom of a long avenue. It wound uphill through trees and after half a mile opened out into a broad gravelled space in front of the magnificent, creeper-covered Georgian house. He stopped in front of the portico, got out and stood for a moment admiring the view. The house was beautifully situated so that it enjoyed a vista which extended to the Isle of Purbeck. The sweeping acres of parkland were studded with judiciously placed copses and single trees.

He mounted the two steps and rang the bell beside the front door. Inside the house he heard a clock slowly strike the half hour. From somewhere beyond the trees came the sound of a tractor. He waited a couple of minutes before ringing the bell again. This time he reinforced it by giving two sharp raps on the knocker. There was no doubt that the house was inhabited by someone who not only had money but did not spare its use on the estate. The driveway was clear of weeds, as were the flower beds along the front of the house. The windows were clean and polished, the

46

paintwork spick and span. He was about to ring the bell for the third time when the front door was opened.

A woman of about fifty was staring at him with a completely non-committal expression. There was neither welcome nor hostility on her face. Even in her flat slippers she was as tall as Peter. Her face was pale and thin, the features sharp and angular.

'Yes? What is it?' Her manner was terse rather than rude. The voice was precise, the accent that of an educated person. He assumed that she was Sir Arnold's housekeeper.

'Could I speak to Sir Arnold Wyatt, please?'

'Have you an appointment?'

'No. I'm afraid I haven't. My name is Matty. Peter Matty.'

She looked him over deliberately, noting his clothes, his shoes, his hands, clean-shaven face and well-cut hair. When she had finished weighing him up she switched her scrutiny to the car. The Jaguar appeared to tip the scales.

'Just a moment, please.'

She left the door ajar. Peter turned his back to it and was admiring the view when he realised that he was being watched. A patch of colour under an aged yew tree at the side of the house caught his eye. He turned his head and saw a little girl standing in the shadow of the tree. She was wearing a spotless sky-blue dress and immaculately white socks and shoes. He reckoned she was about five years old. He smiled at her. She did not return his smile, just went on staring at him with her wide-open, unblinking eyes.

'Sir Arnold will see you.' The housekeeper had returned soundlessly. The front door was held wide open. 'Please come this way.'

He followed her into the hall. When the front door was

closed it seemed dark after the sunlight outside. Only dimly was he aware of the polished floor, gleaming antique chests, the grandfather clock he had heard striking. Ahead he could hear the sound of a sophisticated high-fidelity system. The music was a Beethoven piano concerto. It was switched off as he crossed the threshold of the room the housekeeper indicated.

He had to descend a couple of steps to enter Sir Arnold Wyatt's study. It was a large room lined with panelling and well-filled bookshelves. There were leather, button-upholstered armchairs and a couple of comfortable settees. On the walls were classical oil paintings in gilded frames. Books were scattered everywhere. Peter noticed that a section of the shelves had been adapted to take long-playing records. Three or four LP's lay on a table near the fire-place. He recognised his brother's photograph on one of them.

Sir Arnold was just moving away from the record player placed under one of the windows. Peter judged him to be in his early sixties. He was well preserved and his whole manner was that of a man who has had a successful career in one of the more exacting professions. His face was scholarly but alert. He subjected Peter to a swift scrutiny. The housekeeper had melted away into the dark hall.

'Mr Matty?' Sir Arnold's voice was friendly, but he did not offer to shake hands.

'Yes.'

'I'm Sir Arnold Wyatt. What can I do for you, sir?'

'I'm a friend of Mrs du Salle's,' Peter explained, expecting that this would break the ice. 'I expect she mentioned my name to you yesterday afternoon. I lent her my car and I was wondering why she abandoned it.'

'Mrs du Salle?' Sir Arnold repeated the name without any change of expression.

'Yes.'

'I'm sorry, Mr Matty, but I think there's some mistake. I don't know anyone of that name.'

'But she came here yesterday afternoon. You invited her for the weekend.'

'I did?' Sir Arnold's raised eyebrows expressed polite disbelief.

'Yes.'

'But I've never heard of Mrs du Salle.' Puzzled, he waved Peter to one of the leather armchairs. 'Sit down, sir.'

Peter sat down. Sir Arnold took the chair by the fireside. 'Now, would you be kind enough to explain what this is all about?'

'I've told you. I lent Phyllis du Salle my car and I—'

'Yes, I know!' For the first time there was a hint of irritation in the man's urbane manner. 'You said that.'

'She married a friend of yours,' Peter explained patiently. 'A very close friend—Norman du Salle.'

'I'm sorry, sir.' Sir Arnold shook his head. 'The name doesn't—'

'Look, you must have heard of Norman du Salle,' Peter insisted with exasperation. 'You looked after him when his parents died. Then he became a journalist and emigrated to America—'

'I'm sorry,' Sir Arnold cut in with acerbity, 'but I haven't heard of any of these people. And if you'll forgive me saying so, I haven't heard of you either. Now, what's all this about and who are you exactly?'

'My name is Peter Matty. I'm a book publisher.' Peter nodded towards the record sleeve on the table. 'And if you haven't heard of me you've certainly heard of my brother.'

'Claude Matty?' For the first time there was warmth in the other man's voice. 'He's your brother?'

'Yes.'

'I'm a great admirer of your brother's, Mr Matty,' Sir Arnold said, smiling. 'He's given me a lot of pleasure over the years. He has indeed!'

Peter took out his wallet, extracted one of his cards and handed it to his host. Sir Arnold held it at arm's length to read it. 'Matty Books. Why, yes, of course.'

He studied Peter with a more friendly expression. 'Forgive me if I seemed a little abrupt just now, but— well, to be frank, I'm utterly bewildered by what you've just told me. Who is this Mrs du Salle? And what gave you the idea that she was a friend of mine?'

'I met her on a plane coming back from Geneva. We got talking. She told me that it was her first visit to England and that she was very much looking forward to meeting you.'

Sir Arnold's brows knit and he shook his head.

'She said you were a very close friend,' Peter continued. 'A very dear friend of her late husband.'

'But this is nonsense! I assure you I've never even heard of the lady. But please go on, Mr Matty.'

'I have a boat in Poole Harbour and since I was coming down here for the weekend I offered to bring her down.' Convinced now that he was on a false scent Peter shrugged his shoulders. 'And that's about it—except that I lent her my car to drive over here.'

'When was this?'

'Yesterday afternoon. My car was returned to me early this morning.'

'By Mrs du Salle?'

'No. By the police. Apparently she left it in a deserted lane not far from here.'

Sir Arnold rose and went to stand with his back to the empty fire-place.

'Well! This is really quite extraordinary. I just don't understand it. You say you met the young lady coming back from Geneva?'

'Yes. I'd been to a concert given by my brother.'

'And you—got friendly with her?' A fresh idea had struck Sir Arnold. 'Did she—? Forgive my asking, but did she borrow money from you?'

'Good heavens, no!' Peter laughed. 'She wouldn't even let me take her out to dinner.'

Again the older man shook his head in bewilderment.

'Well, this is quite beyond me. I must confess I really don't know what to say to you. I just can't imagine what this young lady was up to.'

Peter could not bring himself to believe that this distinguished man was blatantly lying to him, though he was now just as much at a loss as his host. He rose to his feet.

'My apologies for troubling you. I've taken up quite enough of your time.'

Sir Arnold did not contradict him. He put out an arm to shepherd him towards the door.

'If your brother ever finds himself in this part of the world, Mr Matty, I'd be more than delighted to make his acquaintance.'

Mrs Cassidy, the housekeeper, did not reappear and it was Sir Arnold himself who saw his guest to the door. When he had waved a short farewell he went back into the house and shut the door. Peter took his time about getting

51

into the car and starting the engine. As he swung down the drive he saw the little girl again. She was standing in the shade of a copper beech, still staring at him impassively. But now he saw that she was holding a doll—a doll dressed in Tyrolean costume.

5

Peter remained at Poole for ten days, hoping that Phyllis would contact him, either directly or through Mrs Frinton. But no message came and there was no report in the local papers to confirm his worst fears that she'd met with some mishap. In the end he decided that he had in some way unwittingly offended her by urging her to stay with him on the yacht and had accepted his offer of the car as a rather elaborate way of giving him the brush-off.

He returned to London, wondering if she might try to contact him there. He did his best to immerse himself in his work but he could not drive the thought of her out of his mind. If there had been *some* message, *any* message. The latest symptom of his state of mind was that several times he thought he had spotted her in a crowd. That incident in the restaurant on the day that his brother turned up so unexpectedly from Stockholm had been the nearest he had come to making a complete fool of himself by accosting a total stranger.

'My God!' Claude exclaimed, when he had heard Peter's tale. 'You really have fallen for her, haven't you? There's nothing like a confirmed bachelor—'

'For making a fool of himself.'

'That's not quite what I was going to say. I suppose she really was staying at the Connaught?'

'Yes. I've checked with them. She was staying there all right, but she left no forwarding address.'

'What about Max Lerner? Have you spoken to him about this? Didn't she tell you they'd once met?'

'Yes. But he doesn't remember meeting her.'

'Well.' Claude put his hands behind his head. 'The only thing I can suggest, dear boy, is—try and forget the whole episode. But that doesn't help very much, I'm afraid.'

Peter came away from the window to help himself to another cigarette. He had smoked four while he had been giving Claude his account of the past five weeks. He had always enjoyed the occasional cigarette but Claude had never known him chain-smoke like this. He resisted the temptation to make some comment as Peter lit up yet again.

'When do you propose going down to the boat, Claude?'

'This evening—if that's all right with you.' Seeing Peter's surprise, he explained. 'I know what will happen if I stay in Town. The phone will start ringing and I'll get involved, which means I won't have a moment to myself.'

'Yes. I'm sure you're right,' Peter agreed, his mind on his own problems rather than Claude's. 'I'll join you on Saturday morning. Friday night, if possible.'

It was nearly midnight when Peter returned to his flat in Sloane Court. Dinners with Max Lerner tended to become long drawn-out sessions. Max had had plenty to drink and was in ebullient form when the taxi they were sharing dropped Peter in Lower Sloane Street.

'Thanks for the dinner, old boy,' he said in a slightly slurred voice. 'And the cheque. My ex-wife—wives, I should say—will be most grateful.'

It was a short walk to the entrance to the mansions in Sloane Court where he lived. He used his first key to gain admittance to the ground floor hall. As his flat was on the first floor he did not bother to take the lift, but ran up the stairs two at a time. As he entered the flat his foot brushed one of the inevitable cards advertising a cut-price taxi service. He switched on the hall light and propped the card on a ledge with half a dozen others.

He wandered into his sitting room, which was bright and modern. It had what is politely called a lived-in appearance. Most of the chairs and the settee had books lying on them. The ashtrays were full of cigarette stubs and the smell of stale tobacco smoke was still in the air. An empty glass stood beside a whisky bottle on the coffee table.

He switched the radio on. The sound of the late-night Radio 2 programme boomed out from the hidden stereo speakers. Loosening his tie and taking off his jacket, he moved towards the door leading to his bedroom. It was a great deal more untidy than the sitting room, with clothes thrown on the chairs and bed. Another pile of books was on the bedside table. He threw his jacket and tie onto the nearest chair and picked up the top book. It was one of his own publications. The jacket, he thought, was really not bad.

He took off his shirt, put on a silk dressing gown and drifted into the bathroom. He switched on the light over the basin and took his toothbrush from the rack. He leant forward to study his reflection in the mirror. Even he could see that he had changed in the last month. His face was much thinner and there were shadows under his eyes.

As he was staring critically at himself a gleam of reflected light caught his eye. He swung round quickly, believing that it had been some optical illusion. But he had been right in his first impression. The bath was filled with water, right up to the level of the escape pipe. Its surface was still moving. Floating on it was a child's doll.

It was dressed in Tyrolean costume and was floating on its back, made buoyant by its plastic limbs. Its chubby arms were extended from its sides. It wore an inane smile on its scarlet, baby lips and the bright blue eyes stared placidly at the ceiling. Unless he was much mistaken it was a replica of the doll he had seen in the hands of the little girl at Forest Gate Manor.

He was so astonished that he stood staring at it and only gradually came to realise that the buzzer of the entry-phone was sounding. He went out to the hall and picked up the receiver.

'Who is it?'

'Mr Matty?' a blurred voice inquired.

'Yes.'

'Could you spare me a few moments, sir? My name is Seaton. Detective-Inspector Seaton.'

'Yes, of course. Come on up. It's the first floor.'

He had time to put on his shirt and jacket before the bell rang. He opened the door to find a tall, serious man of about thirty-five standing on the mat. As he was wearing plain clothes it was evident that he was a CID officer. He showed Peter his identity card and was ushered into the sitting room.

'Sorry to trouble you at this time of night, sir.' His eyes were roaming round the room with the instinctive observation of his profession.

'That's all right,' Peter said. The arrival of a police officer at the very moment when he had discovered the doll had shaken him. He had a premonition that this was the start of a very unpleasant chain of events.

'I understand you have a Jaguar, sir?'

'Yes, I have.'

'Registration number NPE 277W?'

'That's right.'

'Then I rather imagine this is yours, sir.' The inspector produced a car key from behind his back. 'It has the number on it.'

As he took the key Peter was reminded of the young officer on the quay at Poole. But this was a different key. Attached to it was a leather tag and a metal ring. The tag bore the name of the agent he had bought the car from. This was the key he had left in the car when he lent it to Phyllis. He turned it over in his hand.

'Yes, this is mine.'

'Did you lose it, sir?' The inspector was watching him with an odd expression.

'No, I gave it to someone.' Peter stared into the other man's face, hesitating to ask the obvious question. 'Where did you find it?'

The police officer paused before answering. It was natural for him to create the maximum effect with any startling announcement. There was often something to be learnt from the reactions of his interlocutor.

'A woman was picked out of the Thames near Deptford this afternoon. That key was in her possession.'

The statement, terrible as it was, left Peter completely numb. He did not feel anything.

'Picked out of the—You mean, she's dead?'

'Yes, sir.' The man was still watching his face. 'She'd been shot and her body dumped in the river.'

Peter's mind was racing. He was back in the cocktail bar of the Connaught Hotel, listening to Phyllis telling him how she had discovered a doll floating in the bath just before the police had informed her that they had found her husband's body washed up on a beach. Now the exact same thing was happening to him.

'I think you will find her name is du Salle,' he heard himself say, with extraordinary calmness. 'About three weeks ago she borrowed my car and—forgot to return the key.'

Seaton shook his head. 'No, sir. We've established who she is. We just wondered if by any chance you could add anything further to our information.'

He saw Peter rock on his feet and realised that he could easily push this cat and mouse game too far.

'Her name is Braithwaite,' he said. 'Linda Braithwaite. She's an American.'

6

Peter shortened his week by a day and followed Claude down to Dorset on the Friday. But instead of going directly to Poole he made a detour to Heatherdown.

Sir Arnold Wyatt, though mildly surprised to see his visitor again, received him more affably than on the first occasion. He even went so far as to offer him sherry. Not until he had poured them each a glass of fino from a crystal decanter and they were seated in the leather armchairs did he inquire the purpose of this visit.

'Well, did you find the young lady you were looking for?'

'No, I'm afraid I didn't.' Peter tasted his sherry, which was pleasantly dry.

'I was talking to Mrs Cassidy, my housekeeper, after you left and we really could not think who she could possibly have been. It really was an extraordinary story.'

'Sir Arnold, when I was last here I noticed a little girl playing on the lawn.'

Sir Arnold smiled with pleasure. 'Yes. That was Jane, my grand-daughter.'

'She had a doll in her arms. A rather pretty little doll.'

'Yes, that's very likely.' Sir Arnold was puzzled by Peter's terse manner. 'I know the doll you mean.'

'Has she lost it, by any chance?'

'Lost it?' Sir Arnold's carefully schooled features be-trayed his surprise at what he obviously considered to be an impertinent question for a stranger to ask. 'The doll, you mean?'

'Yes.'

'I don't think so.'

'Because if she has, I think I've found it.'

Peter put his glass down and reached for the little zip-up holdall which he had placed beside his chair. He unfastened it and produced the Tyrolean doll. Sir Arnold was watching him with an amazement which increased when he saw the doll.

'Yes, that's Jane's! Where did you find it? On the drive?'

'No. I found it last night. Someone left it in my flat.'

'In your flat?' Sir Arnold said with polite disbelief. 'But why on earth should anyone do that?'

'I don't know. I can't imagine why. I simply went into the bathroom before going to bed and there it was.'

Sir Arnold stood up and came over to take the doll from Peter.

'This looks remarkably like Jane's,' he murmured, examining the doll both front and back. 'Yes, I'm sure it is. I'll have a word with my housekeeper.'

He went to the telephone table where a black internal instrument stood beside the white Post Office one. He pressed a button and waited for half a minute.

'Mrs Cassidy. Would you send Jane along to the study, please? Yes, straight away.'

As he replaced the phone Peter asked: 'Does your little grand-daughter live in Heatherdown?'

Before answering Sir Arnold handed the doll back to Peter. He picked up his glass and took a sip. 'She lives here, Mr Matty, with me. Her parents are dead.'

'Oh! I didn't realise that.'

'No, of course not.' Sir Arnold's matter-of-fact tone

60

made it clear that he did not intend to show any emotion. 'Why should you? My daughter and her husband were killed in a plane crash.'

'I'm sorry.'

'As a matter of fact this doll,' he held it out at arm's length to eye it again, 'if it's the one we think it is, arrived for Jane the very day the accident happened. It was Jane's birthday and her father, my son-in-law, sent it from Vienna.'

Peter was at a loss for words. The doll, inanimate as it was, seemed all at once to be an object of ill omen. To break the silence, he said, 'It must be a great responsibility looking after a little girl.'

'It is, and I'm not getting any younger.' Sir Arnold sighed and finished his sherry. 'But she's a delightful child and fortunately Mrs Cassidy is devoted to her.'

He picked up the decanter and raised his eyebrows at Peter. Peter shook his head. Sir Arnold refilled his own glass.

'You probably read about the accident. It happened at Innsbruck. I was very devoted to my daughter, Mr Matty. She was an only child.'

Very briefly the older man's defences were lowered. His loneliness showed in the sag of his mouth and the sadness of his eyes. But his whole face lightened when there came a gentle tap on the study door. He went to open it. The little girl Peter had seen on the lawn came shyly into the room. She was holding a Tyrolean doll, the exact replica of the one in Peter's hand.

Sir Arnold smiled at Jane, then stopped and gently took the doll from her. He straightened up and turned to Peter.

'We appear to have been mistaken, Mr Matty.'

★

'Sorry about the meal, Claude. It hasn't been very good, I'm afraid.'

'Not to worry,' Claude said equably. 'The coffee's good.'

'We'll drive into Heatherdown tomorrow and do some shopping. I saw a good delicatessen in the High Street.'

The brothers were sitting at the slung table in the small but snug cabin of *First Edition*. On their plates were the left-over remains of Peter's attempt at bubble-and-squeak. They were brooding over large cups of steaming black coffee. The doll lay at the end of the table beside the percolator. Peter had lit the inevitable cigarette and was drawing the smoke into his lungs as if it was the elixir of life.

'You know,' Claude remarked, his sensitive fingers toying with the sugar spoon, 'I still can't understand why you didn't tell that inspector about the doll.'

'I didn't tell him because I thought I knew who it belonged to. Also, it was such a complicated story that I just didn't think he'd believe me.'

'But someone broke into your flat, Peter!'

'No one *broke* into the flat. Whoever planted the doll must have had a key and simply let himself into the apartment.'

'How many keys are there?'

'Two. I've got one and Mrs Galloway, my daily, has the other.'

'Has she still got it?'

'Yes, she has. I checked.'

'You haven't given anyone else a key?' Claude asked the question with some diffidence. 'Recently, I mean.'

'No, I've just told you, there's only—' Peter stopped, realising what Claude was getting at. As the latter had feared, he reacted angrily. 'Look, Claude, I told you the truth about Phyllis du Salle!'

Claude gave him a frank look. 'The whole truth?'

'Yes, the whole truth! I didn't sleep with her and I didn't give her a key to my apartment, if that's what you're thinking.'

'All right, old boy.' Claude put up a placating hand. 'Fair enough. But the thing I find very puzzling is that you found the doll—*a doll*—under almost exactly the same circumstances as Mrs du Salle.'

'Yes, I know.'

'Have you examined it?'

'Examined it? What do you mean?'

'Well—have you looked inside it?'

Peter stared at him. 'No, I haven't.'

'Don't you think it might be a good idea if you did?'

Peter picked up the doll and scrutinised it with new interest.

'You think there might be something hidden inside it?'

'It's possible. If there is it could explain a great deal.'

'Well, we'll soon find out.'

Peter thrust the doll at Claude. He got up and went into the galley. When he came back he was holding a sharp kitchen knife. He pushed the plates and cups to the end of the table to clear a space, sat down and took the doll from his brother.

Claude watched in silence as he snipped away the Tyrolean outer costume, exposing the demure knickers. These too he removed, together with the socks and tiny shoes. The naked doll with its pink plastic body was obscene but sexless. Surprisingly it had quite a fat tummy. Claude winced as Peter made a brutal incision down the front of the effigy and began to disembowel it, gouging the wadding out with the point of the knife.

'There's nothing here, I'm afraid,' Peter was saying, when Claude put a hand on his arm.

'Listen! There's someone coming.'

They both froze, listening as they had so often done in boyhood when they had been caught rifling the food cupboard, or pinching windfalls from the neighbour's orchard.

'Anybody at home?' a voice called from the deck above.

'It's Mrs Frinton,' Peter said with relief. He called, 'Come along down, Mrs Frinton.'

She came gingerly down the steps into the cabin. She had put on her hat and was wearing a tweed coat more suitable for winter than summer.

'Sorry to disturb you, Mr Matty.'

'That's all right. What can we do for you? Oh—I think you know my brother.'

'Yes, we have—'

Mrs Frinton was coming forward with a smile when she stopped dead and her jaw dropped. She had seen the doll lying spread-eagled on the table, its clothes torn off and its stomach ripped open.

'—we have met. Good evening, Mr Matty. I heard you were down here. Nice to see you again.'

'Thank you, Mrs Frinton. You're looking just as bonny as ever.'

'Well, I'm not too bad, sir, all things considering.' She finally dragged her eyes from the doll and gave both Claude and Peter a quick, wary look. The spectacle of the disembowelled figurine had for the moment put the reason for her visit out of her mind, but now she remembered. 'There's been a message for you. That friend of yours telephoned at last.'

'Friend of mine?' Peter rose from the table. 'You don't mean Mrs du Salle?'

'She didn't leave her name but I'm sure it's the same lady. She wants you to ring her back. I've got the number somewhere.' Peter exchanged a glance with Claude as she began to hunt through her pockets. 'Oh, dear, what did I do with it? Ah, here we are!'

She produced a piece of paper twice folded. Peter took it from her and read the number. 'Heatherdown 98064.'

'That's right, dearie.'

'What else did she say?'

'She asked me if you were staying down here. I said I wasn't certain but I felt sure you'd be coming because I'd heard your brother was already here.'

Peter took Mrs Frinton's elbow and began to propel her towards the stairway. 'Claude, I'll be back in ten minutes. Come along, Mrs Frinton, I want to use your phone.'

It was long after closing time. Mrs Frinton let Peter in through the door of the shop and turned on the strip light to illuminate the rapidly darkening interior. Peter went straight to the telephone. Holding the paper up so that he could see it clearly he carefully dialled the prefix for Heatherdown and then the number. The number rang quite briefly before a woman answered.

'Hello? Who is it?'

The curt, precise voice sounded familiar but he did not immediately place it.

'Is that Heatherdown 98064?'

'Yes. Who is calling?'

'Could I speak to Mrs du Salle, please?'

'I beg your pardon?'

'You are Heatherdown 98064?'

'Yes.'

'Well, could I speak to Mrs du Salle, please.'

There was a short silence. Then the woman said, 'I think you've got the wrong number. Who is that speaking?'

'My name is Matty. I'm a friend of Mrs du Salle and I have a message to ring her on this number. So, may I please speak to her?'

After a pause the woman said, 'Will you hold on?'

He waited for several minutes, long enough for Mrs Frinton to take the pin out of her hat and hang it up with her overcoat in the little passage leading from the shop to her sitting room.

'This is Sir Arnold Wyatt speaking. Can I help you?'

Peter gave a start, hearing the familiar voice loud in his ear. 'Sir Arnold?'

'Yes. Has something happened, Mr Matty? My housekeeper seems a little confused . . . Hello?'

Peter recovered his voice. 'I—I received a message asking me to ring your number.'

'There must be some mistake. I left no message for you. Are you sure it was this number?'

'Yes.'

'Who is it you wanted to speak to?'

'Er—Mrs du Salle.'

'Mrs du Salle!' Sir Arnold was holding onto his customary well-bred patience with an effort.

'Yes. She telephoned a friend of mine and—left a message for me to ring her back.'

'At this number?'

'Well, I thought so, yes.'

'Mr Matty, either your friend has got hold of the wrong number or someone is quite deliberately trying to make a fool of you. Frankly, in view of what's happened I'm inclined to think the latter. Now, if you'll excuse me I'm listening to a particularly good concert.'

'I'm sorry to—' Peter began, but the receiver at the other end had been replaced. Slowly he hung up his own instrument on the wall fitting.

Mrs Frinton's outline could be seen at the end of the passage. She had been pretending to rearrange the coats hanging there while cocking an ear to the telephone conversation. Realising it was finished she came back into the shop.

'Mrs Frinton.' Peter held up the piece of paper. 'Are you sure you did not make a mistake with this number?'

'I'm quite sure,' she affirmed, taking no offence and nodding vigorously. 'I took it down straight away. Didn't you get hold of your friend?'

'No, she wasn't there.'

Mrs Frinton put on an expression of sad commiseration. 'Well, there was no mistake about the number, dearie. I promise you, I wrote it down straight away.'

In Heatherdown next morning Claude set off to find an off-licence where he could buy some decent wine, while Peter went to stock up at the delicatessen. They met half an hour later at the car, each carrying two heavy plastic bags. Peter had parked the Jaguar in a small square opposite an old-fashioned café with bow windows. A sign was propped outside which read, 'Morning coffee being served.'

Peter opened the boot and they stowed their purchases inside.

'Do you feel like a coffee?' Claude suggested, indicating the board.

'Yes, why not? The only thing I've still got to get is

cigarettes. Tell you what, you find a table and order coffee and I'll join you inside.'

Claude nodded and headed for the café. Peter crossed the road and retraced his steps up the High Street. He had noticed a tobacconist a little way back but with both hands full he'd decided to return for his cigarettes. The shop was just beyond the photographer's, outside which he had stopped to ask directions on his first visit to Forest Gate Manor. As he walked by, Peter noticed a sign in the window:

MORTIMER BROWN. PHOTOGRAPHY
ANNIVERSARY EXHIBITION

The display consisted of wedding groups, local events, carefully posed children and babies, even a few pets. He glanced casually at the photographs as he went past. He had not taken more than three steps when he stopped dead in his tracks. He went slowly back, feeling certain that he was about to be disappointed as he had been so many times in the past three weeks.

He stared at the large portrait which had been placed in the centre of the display, between two wedding groups. This time there could be no mistake. The face in the silver frame was that of Phyllis du Salle.

A bell pinged when a couple of minutes later he opened the photographer's door. Entering the shop he found that the anniversary exhibition continued inside. The walls and display cabinets were filled with examples of Mortimer Brown's work over the past thirty years. It had not been confined to groups and portraits. There were landscapes and pastoral scenes as well as an interesting series of close-ups of moths and butterflies. Mortimer Brown was evidently highly versatile.

Peter was examining an enlarged photograph entitled 'self-portrait' when the curtain dividing the shop from the photographic studio was parted. He recognised the man who came through as the subject of the portrait—some twenty years on. Mortimer Brown was in his early fifties, tall, thin and neatly dressed in a grey suit. The face had sunk since the self-portrait had been taken. He now wore spectacles and the top of his head was balding. He gave the prospective customer a smile which was intended to be friendly and reassuring, but Peter felt that he was already seeing him as a photographic subject, calculating angles, lighting and exposures.

'Good morning.'

'Good morning. I've just been admiring your display.'

'Thank you, sir.' Mortimer Brown came round the edge of the counter and ran his eye proudly over his exhibits. 'That's very kind of you. It's our anniversary exhibition. My father established the business thirty years ago next month. Can I assist you in any way?'

'Yes. I think perhaps you can. A friend of mine is getting married shortly and he's asked me to arrange for the photographs.'

'Is it a local wedding?'

'Yes. I suppose you'd call it local,' Peter improvised. 'Canford Cliffs.'

'That's certainly within our area. We'd be delighted to help you.' He picked up a folded printed sheet from the counter. 'Perhaps you'd like to take one of our brochures?'

'Thank you.'

'That'll tell you what you want to know.' He smiled. 'Which is mainly the price, I imagine.'

'I don't think he'll be too fussy about the price providing the photos are—up to scratch.'

'He'll have no need to worry about that, sir.' The photographer made a gesture towards the tiered shelves in the window, where the photographs stood with their backs to the shop.

'I was particularly taken by those two wedding groups in the centre.' Peter moved towards the display. Mortimer Brown followed him.

'Ah, yes,' he said, gazing down with satisfaction at the pictures Peter indicated. 'This one is a wedding we covered in—when was it?—July, I think. Rob Milton. He's Chairman of the local council. It was a dreadful day. Rained solidly most of the time. But you'd never think it from the photograph, would you?'

'No, you certainly wouldn't,' Peter agreed. Then he nodded casually at the portrait between the two groups. 'Do I recognise that girl? I seem to have seen her before somewhere.'

'You could have seen her, sir. But not recently, I'm afraid.' Mortimer Brown shook his head gravely. 'She and her husband were killed in an air crash about two years ago. A dreadful business, terribly sad. She was Sir Arnold Wyatt's daughter.'

7

Peter found Claude sitting at a table beside the bow window of the café. The house was one of the oldest in Heatherdown. There were low beams which had done service as ship's timbers before they had been reused for building in Tudor times. At one end of the room was a deep inglenook. The place was three-quarters full, mostly with Heatherdown ladies taking a respite from shopping. Claude had a cup of steaming coffee in front of him and there was a plate of chocolate biscuits in the centre of the table. He put down the newspaper he was reading when he saw Peter come in.

'What's the matter? You look as if you'd seen a ghost.'

'I think I have.'

Peter sat down and immediately began to open the packet of cigarettes he had bought. He twisted round in his seat to look for a waitress.

'I've ordered for you,' Claude explained. 'She's just bringing it.'

Peter lit his cigarette in the quick, nervous way that had become his habit of late. A stout, pleasant-faced woman in a white apron brought a cup of creamy coffee and put it in front of him with a smile. He took a grateful sip. Claude, who could see that his brother had suffered some kind of shock, waited patiently for the explanation.

'There's a photographer's just up the road. Mortimer Brown.'

'Yes,' Claude said, 'I noticed it.'

'Did you look in the window?'

'No. Why?'

'If you had you'd have seen a photograph of Phyllis du Salle.'

'Good God! Are you sure?'

'Absolutely sure. But that's only part of the story.' Peter was keeping his voice down. He glanced round to see if anyone else was near enough to overhear the conversation, then leant forward with his elbows on the table. 'I went into the shop and talked to Brown. He told me it was a photograph of Sir Arnold Wyatt's daughter.'

'But you told me about Wyatt's daughter,' Claude pointed out, his brow creasing. 'You said she had been killed in an air crash two years ago.'

'That's what Wyatt told me.'

'Then you must have been mistaken about the photograph.'

Peter put a second lump of sugar in his coffee. 'The photograph in the window is of the girl I brought down here three weeks ago. The girl you saw in Geneva. I'm absolutely sure of that.'

'Then obviously Brown made a mistake,' Claude said reasonably. 'That's the only explanation.'

'He appeared to be in no doubt about it, Claude. He said it was Wyatt's daughter as soon as I asked him. He even mentioned her husband and talked about the accident.'

The waitress came and tactfully placed a folded bill on the table beside Claude. He unfolded it and glanced at it idly. 'Do you know what I think you ought to do? Talk to Wyatt about this. Tell him about the photograph and ask him if it really is his daughter.'

'That could be difficult.'

'Why difficult?'

'I've already called on him twice and rung him up once. The last time we spoke he was very abrupt. I'm sure he thinks I'm—well, a little odd, to say the least.'

Claude rubbed his chin thoughtfully with two fingers. 'Didn't you tell me he was a fan of mine?'

'Wyatt? Yes, he is.'

'Then supposing you use me as an excuse and we both drop in on him?'

When Mrs Cassidy opened the door it was evident that she was just about to go out. She was wearing a silk scarf over her head and a light-weight belted mackintosh. When she saw Peter a wary and defensive expression came over her face and she stiffened visibly. It was more than likely that her employer had warned her that the apparently respectable owner of the white Jaguar was becoming a nuisance.

'Good morning, Mrs Cassidy!' Peter greeted her in his brightest and most friendly voice. 'Do you think we might have a word with Sir Arnold?'

Mrs Cassidy was distinctly doubtful, but the presence of Claude helped. Without making any effort to do so he somehow managed to look distinguished—not the sort of person you turn away from any door.

'I'm afraid he's rather busy at the moment, but—if you'll wait a minute.'

She did not quite close the door. As her footsteps receded in the hall they could hear Wyatt's voice calling from the back of the house.

'Who is it, Sheila?'

'It's Mr Matty.'

'Oh!'

This time there was no invitation to come into the study. Wyatt came to the door himself, with the evident intention of dealing with Peter Matty once and for all. When he saw that Peter was not alone his expression changed immediately. Claude was easily recognisable from his photographs.

'I'm sorry to trouble you again, Sir Arnold,' Peter was explaining, 'but you did say if my brother was ever in this part of the world—'

'Yes! Yes, indeed!' Wyatt was smiling at Claude, obviously delighted to see him in the flesh. 'I recognised you immediately, Mr Matty. This is a very pleasant surprise. I told your brother I very much hoped to have the pleasure of meeting you one day. Do come in, please.'

Claude, who was accustomed to such adulation, smiled modestly and let himself be shepherded into the hall. Peter followed. As Wyatt led them to the study Mrs Cassidy was standing near the stairs. She was a little put out by what must have been a change of plan. There was no sign of the little girl.

'You go on, Sheila,' Wyatt said. 'I'll meet you later in Heatherdown.'

He ushered them into the study. For once the stereo was silent. The records which had been strewn about on Peter's previous visits had been put away in their appropriate places on the well-catalogued shelves.

'You've given me so much pleasure, Mr Matty, over the years,' Wyatt enthused. 'I think I must have every recording you've ever made.'

'Thank you, Sir Arnold.' Claude nodded his acknowledgement. 'That's very nice to hear. I've just made

74

a new one. I'll make sure my agent sends you a copy the moment it's released.'

Wyatt beamed. 'That's most kind of you. I appreciate it.'

Claude wanted to bring these mutual compliments to an end. He glanced at Peter, giving him his cue.

'I hope you'll forgive me for intruding like this,' Peter began diffidently, 'but something happened this morning which, well—'

Seeing Peter's hesitation, Wyatt remembered his duties as a host.

'Won't you both sit down?'

When all three were seated he turned to Peter, a little resentful that he had taken over the conversation from Claude.

'You were saying, Mr Matty?'

'The last time I was here you told me about your daughter. You said both she and her husband were killed—in a plane crash.'

'Yes,' Wyatt was puzzled by this sudden change of subject. 'That's right.'

'Well, I saw a photograph of your daughter this morning. At least, I was told it was your daughter—'

Seeing Wyatt frown and realising that Peter was making heavy weather of his explanation, Claude chipped in.

'Sir Arnold, did your daughter have her photograph taken by a man called Mortimer Brown?'

'Yes, she did. I remember the day she went to him. As a matter of fact it was my idea. I hadn't got a decent photograph of Pauline and I thought—' Wyatt stopped, looking from Claude to Peter. 'But what's this all about? Why are you interested in my daughter, Mr Matty?'

It was Claude who answered. 'My brother saw the photograph—it's in Mortimer Brown's window.'

'I thought it was a photograph of someone else,' Peter said hesitantly. 'Someone I know. So I went into the shop and made inquiries about it. The photographer told me that it was your daughter.'

'In other words, you were mistaken?' Wyatt's tone was challenging.

'I don't know whether I was mistaken or not.'

'I'm sorry, but I'm afraid I don't quite follow you.'

Claude suggested quickly, 'Could we possibly see a photograph of your daughter, sir?'

'Yes, certainly. By all means.'

Wyatt rose and crossed to an antique chest. He took a large photograph album from one of the drawers. He was opening it as he came back to the group of chairs.

'Mr Brown took several photographs, but this is probably the one you saw.'

He held the album so that both of them could see. Peter stared at it. The shock on his face was evident. The subject of the portrait was a pleasant enough young woman with dark hair and a wide, determined mouth. She had none of the brilliance of Phyllis du Salle.

'Is something wrong, Mr Matty?'

'That's—that's your daughter?' Peter stammered.

'Yes, of course!'

'It's not Phyllis du Salle?' Claude asked Peter.

'No, it isn't. It definitely isn't.'

'Phyllis du Salle?' Wyatt repeated, more perplexed than ever. He withdrew the album and closed it.

'The photograph in the window,' Peter explained, 'was a photograph of the woman I've been looking for—the one I told you about—Phyllis du Salle.'

'And Mortimer Brown told you it was my daughter?'

'Yes.'

'But why on earth should he do that?'

'I can't imagine why.'

A bicycle was propped against the kerb opposite Mortimer Brown's shop. The white Jaguar drew up a few yards further on. Sir Arnold got out from the passenger's seat, tipping it forward so that Claude could emerge from his cramped position in the rear. Out of habit Peter locked the car before following the other two.

'It's the one in the centre,' he called after Wyatt. 'Between the two wedding groups.'

As Peter joined him Wyatt was staring at the photograph. 'But that *is* my daughter! It's an enlargement of the photo I've just shown you.'

Peter stared at the portrait. Wyatt was right.

'But that's not the photograph I saw here this morning! The one I saw was—completely different.'

Wyatt and Claude looked at him in silence. Then they exchanged an uneasy glance. Angered as much by that glance as by the trick which he was sure had been played on him, Peter turned his back on them and marched to the door of the shop. Slightly embarrassed, the other two followed.

The shop was empty. This time the owner seemed not to have heard the bell. After half a minute Peter rapped on the counter impatiently. Another twenty seconds passed before Mortimer Brown came through the curtain, blinking in the light.

'Sorry to have kept you waiting, sir, but I was in the dark room. Can I help you?'

'I called earlier this morning and asked you about—'

'Of course you did!' He appeared to recognise Peter for the first time. 'I beg your pardon. It's coming into the light after being in there.' He spotted Wyatt and gave him an ingratiating smile. 'Oh—good morning, Sir Arnold.'

'Good morning,' Wyatt grunted, unhappy about the whole situation.

'I shan't keep you long, sir.'

'That's all right. I'm with Mr Matty.'

'Oh, I see.' The photographer turned his attention back to Peter. 'It was about a wedding, if I remember rightly?'

'Yes, but that's not why I've called back.'

Mortimer Brown's face expressed polite surprise. Wyatt, accustomed to being in charge of any situation, stepped forward.

'Mr Matty's still curious about the photograph of my daughter—the one in the window. I understand he's already spoken to you about it.'

'Yes, he has. What is it you want to know?'

'Well,' Peter said. 'In the first place I'd like to know why you've changed it.'

'Changed it?'

'Yes.'

'What do you mean, sir?'

'You know perfectly well what I mean,' Peter retorted angrily. 'The photograph in the window isn't the same. It's not the one you showed me.'

'I'm sorry, I don't quite understand.' Brown crossed to the window display and lifted the central portrait from its place. 'I take it you are referring to this photograph?'

'No, I'm not! I'm referring to the photograph you showed me.'

'But this is the one I showed you.'

'You showed me the photograph of a friend of mine—a Mrs du Salle.'

'Mrs du Salle?' Brown shook his head. He looked at Claude and Wyatt as if for guidance. He could not have implied more clearly that he considered Peter was suffering from delusions. Claude came to Peter's rescue.

'Look, let's start at the beginning. My brother asked you about a photograph which was in your window.'

'That's quite right, sir.'

'He asked you who it was and you said it was a photograph of Sir Arnold Wyatt's daughter.'

'That's quite correct.'

'Yes,' Peter interjected. 'But it wasn't that photograph.'

'But it was, sir. Now I ask you, why on earth would I show you a photograph of someone else and pretend it was Sir Arnold's daughter?'

'I can't imagine why. But you did.'

'Are you alone in the shop, Mr Brown?' Wyatt asked, in an effort to be helpful. 'I mean—do you have an assistant?'

'Yes, I do. A Mr Fellowes. I believe you've met him.'

'Well, is it possible that Mr Fellowes could have changed the photograph without your knowing—?'

'No, it isn't!' Brown's patience had cracked. He was annoyed enough now to interrupt Sir Arnold. 'He's away on holiday at the moment. Besides'—to Peter—'no-one changed the photograph. This is the one I showed you. The one we talked about. Damn it all, it's been in the window the whole week!'

Of the three who were listening to this outburst only Peter knew that it was an act, that the photographer was lying. He stared him in the face for a moment, then turned and walked out of the shop.

He had time to unlock the Jaguar before Wyatt and

Claude joined him. It was evident that they had been more than a little disconcerted by the scene in the shop.

'I'm sorry if I embarrassed you,' Peter said to Wyatt.

'Not at all,' Wyatt answered politely. 'In your place I'd probably have behaved in exactly the same way. Obviously there must be a perfectly simple explanation.'

'There is,' Peter was still fuming inwardly. 'He's not telling the truth.'

'But why should Mr Brown lie to you?'

'I don't know why.'

Claude said, 'And why change the photograph in the window? After all, he didn't know you'd be coming back to the shop.'

Peter gave him a wry look. 'In other words, you both think I made a mistake?'

'Well, yes,' Wyatt said, exchanging an uncomfortable glance with Claude. 'To be perfectly honest, we do.'

Peter opened the door on the passenger's side. 'Then there's nothing more to be said. If you jump in, Sir Arnold, I'll run you home.'

'Thank you, Mr Matty. That won't be necessary. I have some business to attend to here and Mrs Cassidy will pick me up.' Wyatt's expression relaxed as he turned to Claude. He held out his hand. 'Goodbye, sir. It's been a great pleasure meeting you. I hope we shall run across each other again some time.'

There was an awkwardness between the two brothers as they climbed into the Jaguar. Neither of them spoke as Peter turned in the small square and headed out of Heatherdown on the road to Poole. Once on the open road he put his foot down, driving as if he was late for an aircraft. Claude fastened his seat belt but made no other comment.

As he slowed down for Poole Peter said, 'I know what you're thinking, Claude.'

'Do you, Peter?'

'You think I'm so obsessed with this girl that I imagined I saw her photograph in the window.'

'I'm afraid you're wrong. That's not what I was thinking. But it's a possibility, I suppose. Perhaps some trick of the light—'

Peter shook his head. 'Brown switched the photographs. Don't ask me why, but he switched them.'

'I'd like to believe you,' Claude said with quiet concern.

'Well, don't look so worried, old boy.' Peter could see Claude's face in the wide-angle mirror. 'I assure you I am not going round the twist if that's what you're thinking.'

The old High Street of Poole was now closed to vehicular traffic. Peter had to make a detour round the outside of the town to reach the little street where Mrs Frinton had her shop. Claude gave him an inquiring look as he pulled up outside the sub-post office.

'I've got to make a phone call,' Peter explained. 'I shan't be more than five minutes.'

Claude watched him as he banged the car door, hurried round the front of the bonnet and pushed open the door of the shop. Everything about his movements suggested tension. That drive back from Heatherdown had been a disturbing symptom of his state of mind.

When Peter entered the shop Mrs Frinton was serving one of the fishermen who used the same harbour as he did. Peter went straight to the telephone. He took out his pocket book and turned up his list of telephone numbers. Holding the book up in front of him he began to dial the number.

'Lines to London are engaged,' a maddeningly calm voice informed him. 'Please try later.'

He banged the receiver back. Behind him the door opened as the fisherman went out.

'I thought your brother looked very well, Mr Matty,' Mrs Frinton observed in chatty tones.

'Yes, he's fine.'

'How long is he staying down here?'

'A week or so,' he answered shortly. 'He works too hard. He needs a holiday.'

'I'm sure he does,' she went on, oblivious to his impatience. 'I only hope it keeps fine for him. The weather report isn't too bad.'

To Peter's relief a woman with a small child came into the shop, diverting Mrs Frinton's attention. He dialled his number again. This time he was successful. The call was answered very promptly. Max must have been expecting a call from someone else. Peter pushed his coins into the slot.

'Hello! Is that you, Max?'

There was a pause while Max tried to place the voice. Then he said tentatively. 'Peter?'

'That's right.'

'Hello, Squire! How are things? Are you in Town?'

'No, I'm in Poole. Max, I'd like to see you. Something's come up.'

'Yes, all right. Is it urgent?'

'It is rather. How are you placed at the moment?'

'Lots of lovely things in the offing, old boy. But as it happens, at this precise moment I'm terrifyingly free.'

'Good. I'll see you this afternoon. Be at my flat at five o'clock.'

'Yes, all right. But what's this all about?'

'I'll tell you when I see you.'

'No,' Max insisted. 'I'm curious. Tell me now.'

'I'm offering you a job. An assignment.'

'A job?'

'Yes.'

'Five o'clock, old boy,' Max agreed with evident enthusiasm. 'On the dot.' The pips were beginning to sound as Peter hung up.

The constraint was still there as Peter rejoined Claude. He could not help feeling resentful that his own brother had been ready to believe the photographer rather than him. He could tell that Claude was curious about the telephone call he had made but he had no intention of enlightening him.

'Sorry to have kept you waiting.'

'That's all right,' Claude reassured him, looking straight ahead.

'I'm afraid I've got to go back to London this afternoon. Something rather important has cropped up.'

'Oh.'

'Do you want to come back with me or would you prefer to stay down here?'

Claude did not answer at once. He was upset not so much by the news that Peter was returning to London as by the way it had been announced and the abruptness of the question.

'I think I'd rather stay down here,' he said after a moment. 'If that's all right with you.'

'Yes, of course.' Peter realised that he was behaving ungraciously and made an effort to be more civil. 'I'm sorry about this, Claude. It really is important.'

'Not to worry. After all, you mustn't neglect your business.'

83

Not quite sure whether he had detected sarcasm in Claude's voice or not, Peter looked at his brother. Claude did not meet his eye. He appeared to be more interested in the woman coming out of the shop with her child. Peter twisted the ignition key. The engine roared into life.

In making his appointment for five o'clock Peter had forgotten that he would be coming into London just as the evening traffic was building up. He had only five minutes to spare as he parked the car in Sloane Court.

The moment he turned the key in the front door of his flat he knew that someone had got there before him. He always double-locked it when he went out.

He entered his little front hall quietly. He could hear a faint rustling sound from the sitting room. He did not close the door behind him, but tiptoed across the hall. As he crossed the threshold of the front room there was a sharp click from inside. He gave the door a sharp push. It slammed back against a table.

'Mrs Galloway!'

The woman spun round, dropping the handbag she had just closed. She had already put her coat and hat on and had obviously been about to depart. They were both equally surprised. It was normally in the morning that she came in to wash up his dirty dishes and clean the flat.

Mrs Galloway was a Londoner who had married a Scot and become a widow after less than five years of marriage. She had brought up two children on her earnings and looked a great deal older than her forty-seven years. She was a thin woman with a permanently anxious expression but was blessed with the patience needed to look after someone as untidy as Peter.

'Oh, Mr Matty!' She had her hand on her heart. 'You did give me a start.'

'Sorry, Mrs Galloway. I didn't think you'd be here.'

'Well, I am a bit later than usual. I thought, as you was staying on that boat of yours for the weekend—'

'I was. But I've got some business to attend to.'

Peter had crossed to his desk and was taking a cheque book out of one of the drawers.

'Oh, that's a shame.' Mrs Galloway was still a bit put out at being surprised in the flat outside her normal working hours. She could not tell whether Peter's strangely hurried and nervous manner was indicative of disapproval or not. 'Well, I'll be off then.'

'Yes,' he said, without even looking up from the cheque he was writing out. 'Thank you, Mrs Galloway. Have a nice evening.'

As she went out into the hall he tore the cheque out of the book and put it in his pocket. Just at that moment the bell rang. Max, as promised, had arrived on the stroke of five.

'Is Mr Matty in?' Peter heard him ask.

'Yes, he's just this minute arrived. Who shall I say—'

'That's okay. He's expecting me.'

The front door closed as Max came breezing into the sitting room.

'Here we are, Squire! Five o'clock, on the dot!'

Max was very spruce in dog-tooth check trousers and a double-breasted blazer. He wore a silk scarf round his neck.

'Hello, Max. Good of you to come. Sit down. What would you like to drink?'

'What are you having?'

'Oh, I'll probably have a Scotch.'

'Then I'll have the same,' Max said with approval.

Peter went to the drinks table behind the door. As he took the stopper off a bottle of Famous Grouse and poured a measure into two glasses Max was watching him with undisguised curiosity.

'Soda?'

'No, just a spot of water. Where did you say you were when you telephoned?'

'Poole. I drove back this afternoon.'

'Especially to see me?'

'Yes. I told you. I've got a job for you.'

'Well, thank goodness for that.' Max grinned as he accepted the glass Peter handed him. 'I thought perhaps you might have changed your mind while I was on my way over here.'

'Why should you think that?'

Max shrugged. 'Oh, no particular reason, but that's the sort of luck I've been having just lately. Frankly, I badly need work at the moment. All I can get.'

'Alimony trouble?'

'You've said it. My wives are at my throat again. All three of 'em.'

Peter took the cheque from his pocket and offered it to Max with a smile.

'Well, maybe this will keep them quiet.'

Max inspected the cheque. His chubby face creased into a broad smile.

'I say! That's pretty generous.'

'Don't worry, you're going to earn it.' Peter raised his glass. 'Skol!'

'Cheers.'

Max took a generous swig of whisky and tucked the cheque away in his hip pocket.

'Well, what is that job?'

86

'Do you remember, about three or four weeks ago, I told you I'd met a girl called Phyllis du Salle?'

'You met her on a plane coming back from Geneva.'

'That's right.'

'I was able to fill you in on her husband—how he disappeared on the way from Marseilles to Corsica.'

'I had a talk with Phyllis after that. She told me about the accident. She also told me about the row she had with her husband the night he was drowned. It was about a doll.'

'Yes, I know. That's what I told you.' Max had put his glass down to light up one of his cigarillos. 'Peter, get to the point. What is it you want me to do?'

'She's disappeared.'

'Phyllis du Salle? Disappeared?'

'Yes, and I've got to find her. I've just got to find her.'

Max lit up and gave Peter a sharp look through the cloud of smoke.

'You really have fallen for this girl, Peter, haven't you?'

'That's the understatement of the year! I just can't get her out of my mind.'

Following Max's example Peter fished out his own cigarettes. The packet had been badly crumpled in his pocket. He broke two matches before he succeeded in getting one going.

'I've certainly never seen you like this before.'

'That's why I need your help, Max. You've just got to help me find her.'

'All right. All right, old boy.' Max sat down. He took a notebook and pen from his inner pocket. 'This isn't exactly my line of country, but we'll see what we can do. Now, how do I start?'

'Well, first of all, I'd like you to make some inquiries— discreet inquiries—about two men.' Peter began to walk up and down the room as he talked. 'Sir Arnold Wyatt and a man called Mortimer Brown. They both live in Heatherdown. Brown's a photographer. He has a shop in the High Street. Sir Arnold's a retired barrister. He lives in a house called Forest Gate Manor, a very lovely house just outside the village.'

'Sir Arnold Wyatt. Mortimer Brown.' Max wrote the names down and added a note. 'Okay. Now what is it you want to know about them?'

'I want to know if, by any chance, they're friends. Close friends.'

8

Claude had been worried about his brother's odd behaviour and a little hurt by his abrupt departure for London without explanation. Phyllis du Salle, to judge from what Claude knew of her, was tailor-made to arouse all Peter's chivalrous instincts. She was undeniably good looking, behaved with a great deal of style, and had surrounded herself with an air of mystery which made her all the more interesting.

However, he was certainly not going to allow her to spoil the first real holiday he'd had for a long time. The boat was an ideal place to relax. To the fishermen he was just another dude amateur. Mrs Frinton knew that he 'played the piano', but she was a devotee of Radio 4 rather than Radio 3 and had no idea of Claude's world-wide renown. To her his main claim to fame was as Peter Matty's brother. Apart from passing the time of day with the fishermen and a few of the regular strollers along the quay, he kept himself to himself. It was blissful to know that on the boat no telephone could possibly ring.

Of course, he would be out of practice but he could put that right with a week's intensive work before his next recital. He had been getting stale from overwork. He could feel this rest doing him good.

On a sunny morning early in the week after Peter's departure he was up on the fore-deck cleaning up after the visitations of the seagulls which liked to perch on the fittings of *First Edition*. He had borrowed a faded pair of jeans and an old shirt from Peter's locker. He was armed with a bucket and mop and, as always when doing rough manual work, was wearing gloves to protect his hands. Brownsea Island, across the enclosed lagoon of Poole Harbour, had the dark green hue of fir trees. To the south, across Parkstone Bay, the hotels and villas of Sandbanks glowed white. A forest of masts in the harbour there showed like the lances of some waiting army. Daring seagulls, planing on the breeze, glided low over the water of the harbour, then gained height to skim over the quay and the boats moored there. From the harbour came sounds of activity—the hum of a diesel engine, the swish of coasters discharging water, the metallic clank of a crane's scoop.

Claude realised that he was drinking all this in and not getting on with the job. He stirred himself, emptied the dirty water from the bucket over the side. He dropped the bucket into the water on the end of a rope and hauled it up again. He had been swabbing the deck vigorously for five minutes when someone hailed him from the quay.

'Good morning!'

It was Sir Arnold Wyatt. He was wearing an angler's trilby hat and an old but well-cut tweed jacket. Under his arm he was carrying a long-playing record, still in the wrapping from the shop where he had bought it.

'Oh, hello! Good morning!'

Wyatt pointed at the rope in Claude's hands. 'Don't let me interrupt you.'

Claude hauled the bucket up and tipped its contents back into the sea.

'I'm glad you have,' he said, smiling. 'I think I'm in danger of overdoing it.'

'You're like me, I expect. Don't take any exercise for

three or four months and then expect to make up for it in a couple of hours. May I come aboard?'

'Yes, of course. I'm sorry, I thought you were just passing.' As Wyatt came across the narrow gangway Claude moved along the deck to join him, pulling the gloves off his hands. 'My brother's in London, I'm afraid.'

'It was you I wanted to see, Mr Matty.' Wyatt took the LP from under his arm and pulled it out of the bag. Claude saw that it was one of his own recordings. 'I was wondering if you'd be kind enough to autograph this LP for me.'

'Yes, of course.'

'It's our church fête next week and they're having an auction. They have one every year and I usually try to find something a little unusual for them.'

'I'm afraid my pen's below, in my jacket. If you'll excuse me—'

'No need.' Wyatt produced a ball-point pen from his inside pocket. 'Here we are, Mr Matty.'

Claude put his gloves down. He took the pen and the LP. He pondered for a moment before writing an inscription. Wyatt read what he had written and smiled his gratitude.

'Oh, that's very nice. Most kind of you. Most kind. The vicar will be delighted with this, I'm sure.'

He carefully slipped the record back into its bag and looked appreciatively round the boat.

'Nice little craft. It's your brother's, I understand.'

'Are you fond of sailing, Sir Arnold?' Claude asked conversationally. Wyatt seemed inclined to linger and chat.

'No, I'm afraid not. I'm no sailor. I get bored so quickly, that's my trouble. Can't wait to get back to dry land and stretch my legs.'

'Yes, I know what you mean. I must confess I enjoy it, but I'm afraid I get very little time for anything these days except work.'

'Yes, I'm sure. I imagine you're both hard workers— both you and your brother.'

'Yes, I suppose we are, really.'

'Your brother's in publishing, I believe?'

The question was casual, but there was a sharper look on Wyatt's face which indicated more than passing interest.

'Yes, he is.'

'Done awfully well, I hear. Only the other day someone was telling me his firm's got offices all over. Paris, Rome, New York.'

'Well—Paris and New York, certainly,' Claude agreed, wondering why Wyatt was waxing so enthusiastic about Peter's business prowess. 'I don't remember Peter saying anything about Rome.'

'No? Well—I must have been mistaken.' Wyatt managed to convey that he did not usually make mistakes about such things. 'Your brother must travel a great deal, Mr Matty.'

'Yes, I suppose he does. But I'm the traveller, I'm afraid. I seem to live out of suitcases these days.'

'Yes, of course.' Wyatt screwed up his eyes against the glare of reflected light as he gazed towards Sandbanks. 'In your profession you would. Still, being a concert pianist must be very rewarding.'

'It has its compensations, certainly.'

It was a curious conversation. The other man's remarks were oblique. There seemed to be another meaning behind them, which was perhaps why Claude answered so non-committally. After staring across the water for a minute Wyatt made up his mind to come to the point.

'Mr Matty, forgive me, but—your brother's called on me three times recently and each time he's discussed a friend of his. A young lady called Mrs du Salle.'

'Yes, I know.' Claude was smiling slightly. 'I can guess what you're thinking. And I can't honestly blame you. But I assure you, Mrs du Salle does exist. She's not just the figment of my brother's imagination.'

'Well, I'm relieved to hear you say so,' Wyatt said, apparently accepting the assurance. 'I must confess I was beginning to wonder.' He tapped the LP. 'Thank you again for this. Very kind of you. I appreciate it.'

He went briskly across the gangplank. Claude watched him as he set off along the quay, a competent and purposeful figure, very well preserved for a man of his age. As he glanced back to check the traffic before crossing the roadway he saw that Claude was still standing there. He raised the hand holding the LP and gave a cheery wave.

Claude put his gloves on again and went back to his bucket and mop. But his mind was not on the job. After ten minutes he gave it up. He went down into the cabin to wash his hands and change his clothes.

It was the busy time of the morning and there were several customers in Mrs Frinton's shop. She was having to divide her attention between those on Post Office business and others who wanted cigarettes, sweets or papers. She knew everybody and kept up a ceaseless good-natured chatter which prevented her customers from becoming impatient at having to wait.

The public telephone was being used by a day tripper who was ringing her neighbour in Salisbury to ask her if she'd go in and make sure she'd turned the gas stove off. She smiled apologetically at Claude as she hung up.

Claude had his coins ready. He dialled Peter's office. To his surprise it was Peter himself who answered.

'Peter Matty speaking.'

'Hello Peter—how are you?'

'Oh, it's you, Claude. I'm all right, old boy. How are you making out? How's the boat?'

'The boat's fine. I'm the one that's suffering. Too much hard work. When are you coming down here again?'

'Probably in a couple of days. I'm not sure.'

'Well, try and make it for the weekend.'

'Oh, I'll be down for the weekend, definitely. If not before.'

Claude cupped his hand round the mouthpiece and lowered his voice.

'I had a visit from a friend of yours this morning.'

'Oh? Who was that? Mrs Frinton?'

'No, Sir Arnold Wyatt. He wanted me to autograph an LP—for charity. It's the church fête and they're holding an auction.'

'Oh, I see.' Peter evidently did not think there was anything remarkable about that. 'What's the weather like down there?'

'Not too bad. A bit windy.' Claude had not telephoned Peter to talk about the weather. He'd hoped that his brother would have recovered from the strange moodiness which had possessed him at the end of the previous week. But his voice was still detached and a little cold. Even on the telephone Claude could tell that he had lost none of his tenseness. 'Are you busy?'

'Yes, we are at the moment.'

A woman pushed past behind Claude, banging him with the bag of groceries she had bought at the supermarket.

'By the way, Peter, have you people got an office in Rome?'

'No,' Peter said, on a rising inflexion. Then he added warily, 'We have agents there but we haven't got an office. We do very little business with Italy. But why this sudden interest in Matty Books?'

'Sir Arnold said someone told him you had an office in Rome and I said I didn't think you had. That's all.'

Peter pondered that.

'Did Sir Arnold say anything else?'

'Nothing of importance. Although I must admit, I couldn't help feeling that the record was just an excuse—'

'An excuse for what?'

'I don't know.' As the pips began to sound Claude said quickly, 'Let me know when you're coming down.'

During the short conversation the number of customers awaiting attention had been reduced to two. The tall man looking over the newspapers had his back to Claude, so he did not immediately realise who it was. The woman at the sweet counter was uncertain about what she wanted. She kept picking up packets in transparent packaging and putting them down again. Mrs Frinton looked enquiringly at Claude.

'What can we do for you, Mr Matty?'

Claude came out of his reverie. 'Oh. A packet of cigarettes, please.'

'Same sort as your brother?'

'No. Have you any Balkan Sobranie?'

'I'll see if I've got some, dearie. But they're in short supply at the moment.'

She disappeared into the little store behind the counter, to the annoyance of the woman who had now decided which sweets she wanted. The tall man, hearing the name

Matty, had turned round. Claude saw that it was the High Street photographer.

'Mr Matty?' the other said diffidently. 'I don't know whether you remember me, sir. Mortimer Brown. We met the other day when your brother—'

'Yes, of course I do.'

'I—I hope you'll excuse me, Mr Matty—' He ran a hand nervously over his balding head. 'I've been thinking about your brother and the misunderstanding over the photograph—'

'You're not the only one,' Claude said with feeling. 'I've been thinking about it too.'

'Yes. Yes, indeed. I'm sure you have.' The photographer glanced at the other customer, but she was showing no interest in their conversation. 'I had another chat with Sir Arnold—we bumped into each other yesterday afternoon. I'm afraid, like me, he's still utterly bewildered by the whole business.'

Disturbed though he was by his brother's behaviour Claude had no intention of taking this man's side against Peter.

'So am I, Mr Brown. And so is my brother, if it comes to that. He just can't understand why the photograph was changed.'

'But it wasn't changed,' Brown insisted, quietly but without rancour. 'I assure you it wasn't. The photograph you saw was the one in the window, the one I showed your brother in the first place.'

Claude stared back at him without comment. Brown was showing an undue sensitiveness about what should have been a trivial matter. He could not help being unreasonably irritated by the photographer's anxiety to justify himself. His irritation was increased by the next remark.

'Mr Matty, I hope you'll forgive me asking this question but— has your brother been ill recently?'

'He had laryngitis about six weeks ago,' Claude said drily.

'No, I didn't mean that. I meant, has your brother at any time—'

'Mr Brown,' Claude interrupted firmly, 'my brother isn't suffering from hallucinations, if that's what you're thinking. He's a perfectly sane, highly respected, extremely successful business man.'

'Yes. Yes, I know.' Brown's eyes blinked unhappily behind their spectacles. 'That's what Sir Arnold told me. Then how do you account for what happened?'

'I can't account for it.' Claude's tone made it clear that it was Mortimer Brown's actions he could not account for.

'This woman—the person your brother's been looking for?'

'Mrs du Salle.'

'Yes. Have you seen her?'

'Yes, but only briefly. I caught a glimpse of her at Geneva Airport.'

'So you have *actually seen her*?' Brown repeated his question with extraordinary emphasis.

'Yes, I've seen her.'

Brown contemplated Claude as if trying to assess his truthfulness. Mrs Frinton's voice broke the tension between the two men.

'Here we are, Mr Matty. That'll be 95p.'

When the hands of the clock moved round to five and Peter had still not rung for her, Mollie got up and went into his office. He was sitting at his desk, critically examining some jacket designs that had come in. The folder of letters

97

which she had brought in an hour ago was still in his IN tray.

It really was too much! She had hoped that a spell down at Poole with his precious boat would have helped him to snap out of the mood he had been in for nearly a month now. But so far from improving things it had made him worse.

'Don't you want these to go off tonight?' she inquired, her bracelets jingling as she indicated the folder. When Mollie was angry her bracelets jingled like the percussion section of a Lilliputian orchestra. Peter was too wrapped in his own thoughts to read the warning signals.

'I don't really know till I've looked at them. Why?'

'I did say I wanted to get off early this evening,' she reminded him with ominous distinctness.

'So you did.' Peter glanced at his watch. 'Good heavens, it's five o'clock already!' He looked up at her contritely. 'I'm sorry, Mollie. Off you go. If there's anything urgent I'll post it myself.'

Disarmed by his concern, she relaxed.

'Thanks, Mr Matty. Oh, I forgot to tell you. Max Lerner phoned while you were out at lunch.'

'Max? I wish you'd told me sooner.' He checked his irritation. This was not the moment for lecturing her on the importance of passing on messages. He'd pushed her far enough already. 'Did he leave any message?'

'He'd like you to call round and see him some time this evening.'

'Did he suggest any time?'

'He said any time after five o'clock.'

'I see. He didn't say anything else?'

'No. That was all. I thought he sounded a little—well, embarrassed.'

When she had gone he took the folder from his IN tray and began to check through the neatly typed letters. Then, changing his mind, he flipped through the pile and picked out three that were urgent. He shelved the rest, inserted the three in their already stamped envelopes and pushed his chair back.

Max must have found out something of significance. That could be the only reason why he had asked him to come round.

Peter disliked the Underground. Even though it was the peak of the rush-hour, he decided to go up to Islington in his own car.

It took him half an hour to reach the Angel and he was in a bad temper as he turned into Islington High Street. Max lived in a block of flats about half way along in an area where Peter knew from experience it was very difficult to park. He turned up a side street just before Max's block and cruised along slowly looking for an empty parking-meter space. They were all occupied. In the end he left the Jaguar on a yellow line and hoped that the traffic wardens had notched up enough bookings and gone home.

Max had chosen a seedy part of Islington to live in. Probably it was the best he could afford after paying alimony to his ex-wives. Peter had to pass a number of run-down houses which had been turned into the premises for small flash-in-the-pan businesses. The pub on the corner was a Victorian relic which had gained notoriety as the birth-place of several punk-rock groups. Crude posters advertising The Snare and Screaming Henry Higgins were plastered on the wall outside.

The block of flats was by far the most respectable building in the area. It even boasted an entry-phone system. Peter stepped round a group of children playing football in front of the entrance. He pressed the button alongside Max Lerner's name and waited. The kids were using the doorway as a goal. The biggest lad took a shot. The ball slammed the wall very close to Peter. He pressed the button again. There was still no reply.

The door of one of the flats on the ground floor opened and a squat, bearded man in shirt sleeves came marching out. His face was scarlet with rage. When they saw him the kids grabbed their ball and ran.

'I warned you kids before!' the squat man shouted. 'I catch you at it again I'll give you a thrashing you'll not forget in a hurry.'

He threw Peter a disgusted look. 'Bloody kids!' he said and went back into his flat.

Peter tried the entry-phone once more, then went into the gloomy hall. A notice 'Out of order' had been hung on the sliding door of the lift. Strongly suspecting that his journey was in vain he began to climb the stairs. Max's flat was on the fourth floor.

His leg muscles were aching as he pushed the swing-door that separated the lift and stair-well from the corridor off which the flats opened. A board with numbers showed him that Max's flat, number 27, was to the right. As he passed number 26 he could hear from inside the throb of a stereo turned up to full volume. Max's door had a little mat outside it and was embellished with a brass knocker. He was about to use it when he realised that the door was ajar. He pushed it open and found himself in a hall which was more of a passage, with the rooms opening off it.

'Max!'

From the room to his left came the sound of a woman's voice speaking in a metallic monotone. He moved towards it, entered what was obviously the sitting room. It was in a state of picturesque disorder with newspapers and magazines littered everywhere, including the floor. The principal piece of furniture was a magnificent couch covered by an imitation bearskin and half a dozen gaily-coloured cushions. The woman's voice was coming from a portable radio on the table.

Beyond the sitting room was a kitchenette in which an electric cooker and the edge of a sink were visible.

'Max!' Peter called again.

Behind him in the hall he heard the front door close with a bang. A few seconds later Max came into the room. He was holding a half-full bottle of milk in his hand. He nearly dropped it when he saw Peter.

'Peter! My goodness, you made me jump.'

'Isn't it a little unwise to leave the front door open?'

'Yes, but I just popped upstairs. Can't stand black coffee.' Max held up the milk bottle. 'Had to borrow this from the young lady in the flat above. I'm always borrowing something off her. Have to cut it out. She's beginning to think I fancy her.'

He grinned self-consciously, then went to turn off the radio.

'My secretary said you wanted to see me.'

'That's right,' Max said evasively. 'Will you have some coffee?'

'Yes—thanks.' Peter accepted the offer, though it was a time of day when he would have preferred something stronger. Max was glad of the excuse to hurry into the kitchenette.

'Do you take sugar?' he called back.

'Just one, please.'

Peter went to lean against the door of the kitchenette.

He watched Max put a spoonful of Nescafé in each of two brightly-coloured mugs and add boiling water.

'Mollie didn't tell me you'd phoned until half an hour ago, otherwise I'd have called you back.'

'Not to worry.' Max handed him one of the mugs.

'Thanks.'

Max picked up his own mug clumsily. The coffee slopped over the edge and he cursed under his breath. As they moved back into the sitting room he was uncomfortable under Peter's inquiring gaze.

'I don't charge for seats, you know,' he said, in a slightly belligerent way.

Peter moved a couple of magazines from one of the chairs and sat down. 'Well? Why don't you tell me and get it over with?'

Max had placed himself so that he was not facing Peter directly. He did not answer.

'Look, Max. I asked you to make certain inquiries for me. If you've found out something unpleasant, something you think I don't want to hear about—that's my problem. Not yours.'

'It isn't that.'

'Well, there's certainly something on your mind. Go ahead. Let's have it.'

At last Max looked at Peter directly. He seemed both ashamed of himself and defiant. He started to say something, but changed his mind. Then he put down his mug of coffee, took a folded paper from his pocket and handed it to Peter.

Peter unfolded it and gave it a brief glance. 'This is the cheque I gave you.'

'That's right. I'm giving it back to you.'

'Giving it back?'

'Yes. I'm sorry, Peter, but I can't accept the job you offered me.'

'But you have accepted it.'

'Then I've changed my mind.'

Peter stared at him. Max was covering his discomfiture by lighting one of his long, thin cigars.

'Why? Why have you changed your mind? You said you needed a job. You told me you badly needed money.'

'Yes, I know I did, Peter, but'—Max got up and went in search of an ashtray to put his match in—'that was before I had this fantastic offer.'

'What offer?'

'There's a new advertising agency opening up. They're going to make films, advertising films, for television. They've—' Max had adopted his most bland and plausible manner—'Well, they've offered me a five-year contract.'

'I see,' Peter said sceptically.

'I was in television originally, you know.' Max hurried on. 'I've always wanted to get back. This offer's so good, I—just can't turn it down.' He gave Peter what was supposed to be a frank look. 'Honestly, old boy, I really can't.'

'When are you due to start?'

'The end of next week. I'm flying out to Copenhagen at the weekend.'

'Copenhagen?'

'Yes, it's an American company but they're based in Copenhagen.'

'How did you hear of this offer?' Peter asked, far from convinced by Max's tale.

'I answered an advertisement about six weeks ago. I forgot all about it and then suddenly, out of the blue, they telephoned me.'

'When?'

'When?' Max had found an ashtray under a newspaper and was holding it in one hand. He needed time to answer the question.

'Yes,' Peter persisted. 'When did they telephone you?'

'Oh. On Tuesday night. Or was it Wednesday? I'm not really sure.' Max saw that Peter was far from satisfied. He spread out his hands in a gesture of appeal. 'Look, I'm awfully sorry about this, I really am. I hate letting anyone down, but—I really have no alternative.'

'Supposing—' Peter said slowly. 'Supposing I make this proposition of mine worthwhile? I mean—really worthwhile?'

'What do you mean?'

'I don't know what these people are offering you, but just suppose I double it. What then?'

The suggestion only appeared to make Max more unhappy than before.

'It—it wouldn't work. It's frightfully generous of you. Bloody generous, in fact, but it just wouldn't work.'

'Why not?'

'I've told you. I want to get back into television.' Max's apologetic manner had given way to something more like aggressiveness. 'Besides, I've got problems here, in London. Three ex-wives. Alimony. The thought of getting away, living in another country, appeals to me right now.'

'Yes, all right, Max. Forget it. There's nothing more to be said.'

Trying hard to keep his temper Peter stood up. He put the cheque in his pocket. He had hardly touched the coffee.

'Thanks for the cheque. And the coffee.'

As he went to the door Max turned his back and stared

out of the window. His mood had again undergone one of those rapid changes.

'Peter, please don't think I'm ungrateful. Please don't think I've forgotten all you've done for me in the past. You've been a damn good friend in more ways than one. I shall—always try and remember that.'

Peter's last impression of Max, before he let himself out, was of the little journalist standing there with his shoulders drooping and all the bounce taken out of him. The smoke from his cigar rose straight for a couple of feet and then was twisted by an unseen air current.

9

A hundred yards before he reached his car Peter could see the rectangular white paper stuck under his windscreen wiper. The traffic warden, moving away from him, had almost reached the far end of the street. She must have been trying to make up her tally of bookings before knocking off for the day.

Swearing silently at Max Lerner, who was the cause of all this, he pulled the form in its cellophane wrapper from the windscreen and shoved it in his jacket pocket. A skinhead in tight jeans and leather jerkin, probably heading for the Victorian pub, grinned with malicious pleasure at seeing the owner of the white Jaguar copping a summons.

He opened the XJS on the central-locking system, slipped behind the wheel and resigned himself to a slow crawl home through the evening traffic.

Conditions were unusually bad that evening. It was nearly an hour later when he let himself into his flat. He felt thoroughly irritated and depressed. He hung his coat up in the hall, went on into the sitting room. It was, by Mrs Galloway's standards, reasonably tidy. She had gathered up the books which he had left strewn about and placed them in neat piles.

He went straight to the drinks table and poured himself a generous Scotch. When he put his hand in his pocket to feel for his cigarettes it encountered Max's cheque and the traffic warden's form. He tore the cheque up into tiny pieces and flung them into the wastepaper basket. He lit a cigarette before flopping into an armchair.

Though he knew that the form would offer him the alternative of paying an instant fine or being summoned he withdrew it from its protective wrapping. There had been talk lately of increasing the fine and he wanted to know how much his abortive visit to Max was going to cost him. A piece of paper which he had not noticed before fell to the floor. It must have been pushed in behind the official forms. He picked it up and unfolded it. The short message had been typed in capital letters:

MRS DU SALLE HAS AN APPOINTMENT WITH HER DENTIST AT FOUR O'CLOCK TOMORROW AFTERNOON—328A HARLEY STREET.

Peter knew that it was hopeless to try and find a parking space anywhere near Harley Street at four o'clock in the afternoon. As he did not want to collect another parking ticket he took a taxi from his office. The driver dropped him opposite number 328A. It was just after four o'clock but that did not worry him. Phyllis was bound to spend at least a quarter of an hour in the dentist's chair.

Number 328A was up a flight of outside steps at the side of number 328. The names of half a dozen specialists were engraved on the highly polished brass plates beside the door. The third one down read: BASIL J. REID. DENTAL SURGEON. There were no other dentists. He rang the bell with a sense of excitement and anticipation. Phyllis must have gone through this very door only a few minutes earlier.

The receptionist who answered the bell wore a white overall and a cosmetic smile of formal welcome.

'Good afternoon,' she said, holding the door open.

Seeing that Peter hesitated to walk straight in, she asked: 'You have an appointment?'

'No, I—that's to say, I believe a friend of mine has an appointment with Mr Reid at four o'clock.'

'Four o'clock?'

'That's right. Mrs du Salle.'

'Ah, yes, of course. Mrs du Salle's appointment should have been at four but it was changed to three-thirty. You've just missed her.'

'Oh. Thank you.'

The receptionist saw that her announcement had completely deflated the visitor. She waited till he had turned away before closing the door on him.

Peter went down the steps slowly and turned towards the Marylebone Road. He had not tried to find an explanation as to how the message had got onto his windscreen, but had simply accepted it as evidence that at least somebody was on his side in his search for Phyllis.

He was about to cross the street at a zebra crossing when he halted. He stopped, wondering whether he had accepted the receptionist's word too readily. Suppose Phyllis's appointment *was* for four o'clock? He was trying to make up his mind whether to go back and question the receptionist further when a taxi coming along Harley Street slowed down, thinking that he was waiting to cross the road. He signalled the driver to carry on. The man, a cheery Cockney, gave him a nod.

As the cab moved forward Peter caught a quick glance of the solitary passenger. He only saw her for a moment, but that was enough. Instinctively he started after the taxi, but it was rapidly gathering speed and he knew that he had no chance of catching it.

Then, at last, the luck turned his way. The traffic lights at the next street junction turned to amber, then red. The taxi braked to a halt. Peter covered the hundred or so yards in a time which would have done credit to a relay racer. He was still twenty yards away when the light changed to green. The taxi began to move forward with the rest of the traffic. Disregarding the other cars he sprinted onto the road, making a frantic effort to overtake his quarry. A slow-moving Mini, which balked the taxi, saved him. In the nick of time he got a hand to the rear door and wrenched it open.

Phyllis du Salle gave a gasp of surprise and fright as he breathlessly jumped in beside her.

'Phyllis, where the hell have you been? I've been looking all over for you!'

She could find no words. She just sat there staring at him, her eyes wide with astonishment.

'Why didn't you come back to the boat that evening?' he demanded. The questions were tumbling out. This was not what he had planned to say, but he was still bewildered by the way things had happened. 'Did I offend you in some way? Didn't you want to see me again?'

'No. I did want to see you again,' she cut in, recovering herself. 'I intended to come back, but—Peter, please leave me alone! Stop the taxi!'

He ignored the pleading in her voice, took hold of her arm. 'You've got to tell me what this is all about. I want to know why you lied to me, why you suddenly disappeared—'

'Please, Peter,' she begged him again. 'Leave me alone.'

'Don't you realise what I've been going through during these past weeks?' The tension that had been pent up inside him was making his voice sound angry. 'Every day—every single day I've thought about you. There hasn't been a moment when you were out of my thoughts—'

At that moment the taxi took a sudden lurch towards the

kerb and stopped with a jerk. Peter was thrown sideways. As soon as his hold of her was loosened Phyllis opened the door on her side. She was half out before he managed to grab her by the arm.

'Phyllis, listen to me! You've got to listen to me.'

'Let go of my arm!'

'Not till you've told me what this is all about.' He tightened his grip.

'I can't tell you. Peter, please! *Leave me alone!*'

The door behind Peter was violently opened. A hand grabbed his coat collar and yanked him backwards, loosening his hold on Phyllis's arm.

'Do as she says, mate.'

As he twisted round to see the irate, determined face of the taxi driver Phyllis jumped out of the cab and ran back up Harley Street. He attempted to follow her but the driver still had a firm hold of his collar.

'Look, you stay out of this. It's none of your business.'

'What goes on in my taxi, mate, is very much my business.'

Desperate at the thought that Phyllis was escaping, Peter wrenched himself from the man's grasp. He was scrambling towards the door on the other side when he saw her handbag on the floor. He picked it up.

'Oh, no you don't!'

The driver grabbed him by the legs and hauled him backwards, clean out of the cab. As he struggled to his feet the driver was trying to pull the handbag from his grasp.

'Don't be an idiot!' Peter protested. 'She's a friend of mine.'

'Friend? God 'elp your enemies!'

Peter gave his adversary a violent push which sent him

reeling back against the side of the cab. But this only incensed the man more and he landed a swinging blow on the side of Peter's face.

With surprising speed a small crowd had collected. In the roadway horns were sounding angrily. Some drivers had slowed down to watch the unusual spectacle of a taxi driver sparring with one of his fares. A couple of middle-aged women with shopping bags were urging the taxi driver on.

Really angered now and with a smarting cheek Peter wanted to settle the fight quickly. He parried the taxi driver's next clumsy swing and thumped him in the solar plexus. As the man doubled up he wrenched the handbag free. He pushed through the ring of people and started to run in the same direction as Phyllis had gone. His eyes were searching the pavement on both sides of the street as he raced back towards the intersection where the traffic lights were. Just as he reached it two police constables came round the corner. They had been alerted by the sounds of commotion in Harley Street.

Their eyes instantly registered the dishevelled figure with the bloodied cheek, clutching a lady's handbag and fleeing from the hue and cry which was now pursuing him. Unwisely Peter tried to swerve round them. They moved with instinctive speed to interrupt him. Cornered against the railings he realised that in his desperation he had cast himself in the role of a common thief.

'You say you knew the lady, sir?'
'Yes. I've already told you that. She was a friend of mine.'
'*Was* a friend of yours?'
'I used the past tense simply because I haven't seen her

111

for some time—that's to say, since she disappeared with my car.'

Peter was standing in front of the reception desk at the police station to which he had been taken after his arrest. The sergeant on duty, a craggy man with close-cut greying hair, was attempting to make some sense of the situation before getting down to taking statements. The two young constables who had brought Peter in were standing behind him. They had also asked the taxi driver and two women who had witnessed the fight to come along and make statements. Surrounded by these six people Peter did not exactly feel that he was among friends.

Peter's last statement had made the sergeant feel that he was getting onto familiar ground.

'I see. So she stole your car, sir?'

'No, not exactly. I—er—lent it to her.'

'You lent it to her and she didn't return it?' the sergeant suggested, holding onto his patience with an effort.

'Yes. I mean, no.' Peter glanced round desperately and met the expressionless gaze of the younger of the two constables. 'No, she returned it—with a note.' He saw the exasperation coming back into the sergeant's face. 'Look, sergeant, I think we'd better forget about the car.'

'Yes, I think perhaps we'd better, sir. Tell me about the handbag.'

'There's nothing to tell. My friend dropped it and all I did was to pick it up.'

'That's not true!' One of the female witnesses cried out, unable to contain herself any longer. Looking round, Peter recognised her as one of the two middle-aged women who had been urging the taxi driver to 'sock him one'. 'He snatched it from her! I saw him do it!'

'You saw nothing of the kind,' Peter told her.

'Oh, yes she did,' said her friend, pushing her red face forward. 'We both saw you.'

Peter appealed to the taxi driver. 'You know damn well that she left it in the taxi when she got out. You know I only intended to go after her with it.'

'All I know, mate, is that you was trying to assault her and she called out for help. That's why I stopped my cab.'

'Just a minute,' the sergeant interposed. 'Was the handbag in his hand when you opened the taxi door?'

'I don't know,' the taxi driver admitted. 'I'm not sure about that.'

'Yes, it was,' the red-faced woman said. 'I saw him with it. It was in his hand. We both saw it, didn't we, Cora?'

'That's right,' Cora agreed vehemently. 'And the look on his face! It put me in mind of—'

'Madam, will you please be quiet!' the sergeant raised his voice to silence her. 'I can't get a word in edgeways.'

The two women subsided into silence. The sergeant opened his book and picked up a pen.

'What was the name of this friend of yours, sir?'

'Mrs du Salle. Mrs Phyllis du Salle.'

'Can you spell that, please, sir?'

Peter spelt the name out and the sergeant wrote it down.

'And her address?'

'I don't know her address.'

The sergeant looked at Peter sadly. 'You—don't know her address? Did you not say she was a friend of yours? Has she a telephone number?'

'I don't know whether—' In his desperation Peter's eye fell on the handbag which had been placed at the side of the reception desk. 'Why don't you look in her handbag?'

'I've already looked, Sergeant,' one of the constables said. 'There's no means of identification.'

The sergeant nodded, as if Phyllis' failure to carry anything in her handbag which would show her identity was somehow confirmation of Peter's evil intent.

'That's that, then. I'm afraid I shall have to book you, sir.'

'Not before I've spoken to my solicitor.'

'Your name, please.'

Peter realised all too well that things looked very bad for him. He knew that he had lost his head on seeing Phyllis again and that he should never have allowed himself to become involved in that brawl with the taxi driver. Nor could he blame the station sergeant for finding his answers to questions totally unsatisfactory. The best he could do now was to keep quiet and wait for his solicitor to sort this all out.

'I insist on telephoning my solicitor.'

'All in good time, sir. Now, if you'll kindly give me your name.'

The two women had edged round beside him, smirking at his discomfiture. He glared at them before answering the sergeant.

'Matty.'

'How do you spell that?'

'M-A-T-T-Y.'

'Initials?'

'P. P for Peter.'

The red-faced woman sniggered. The sergeant reproved her with a glance and turned to the senior constable.

'What time did you pick him up?'

'Ten minutes past four.'

As the sergeant was entering the time on his charge sheet the telephone on the reception desk rang. He put his pen down and picked up the receiver.

'Sergeant Clifford . . . Yes, that's right. Who is that speaking?' Even though the caller could not see him he instinctively straightened into an attitude of respect as he listened. His voice was deferential as he answered, 'Yes, sir . . . Yes, I'm listening.'

There was silence in the bare room as all those present tried to catch the voice that could faintly be heard crackling in the ear-piece.

'Yes, he is,' the sergeant said. His eyes flicked towards Peter. 'I understand perfectly, sir . . . Yes, of course . . . No, not a word, sir . . . Very good, sir.'

He put the receiver down very gently and contemplated it for a few seconds, readjusting his mind to a completely new set of circumstances.

Then he came round from behind the desk and opened the door of an adjoining waiting room.

'If you'd please step in here for a moment—No, not you, Mr Matty.'

As the taxi driver and the two women filed into the little room the sergeant signalled to the two constables to follow them. Then he closed the door. Left alone with Peter he appeared a great deal less sure of himself than when he had been about to charge him.

'Mr Matty.'

'Yes?'

'You're free to go.'

'Free to go?'

'Yes, that's right. There will be no charge. You're dismissed.'

Without looking at him again the sergeant went back behind the desk, crumpled up the charge sheet and closed his book.

Mollie Stafford was debating in her mind whether to ring Peter's flat. It was nearly ten and she had heard nothing from him since he had left the office without explanation at three-thirty the previous afternoon.

She made her mind up and with a jingle of bracelets pulled the telephone towards her and dialled his home number. It was still ringing when the door opened and her employer came in. There was a piece of sticking plaster over a cut on his left cheek and he had dark shadows under his eyes. If she hadn't known that he was going through a period of deep depression she would have suspected that he'd had a wild night out on the town.

She replaced the receiver. 'Good morning, Mr Matty.'

'Good morning, Mollie.'

He pushed his folded newspaper into the pocket of his raincoat, which he was taking off as he went through to his office.

'I've put the mail on your desk. There's quite a collection. And I've left you a list of the people who phoned after you'd gone yesterday afternoon.'

The note of gentle reproof which she had put into her voice was lost on him.

'Oh. Thank you,' he murmured absently.

'There's a letter from Angela Blackwood. She's finished her novel at long last.' Mollie shook her head in mock despair. 'One book every four years. I don't know how on earth she manages to live.'

'I do.' There was a ghost of the old smile on Peter's face. 'She has a fleet of boy friends.'

116

'You must be joking! She has a face like a horse.'

He grinned at her and disappeared into his office, leaving her satisfied that she'd got a smile out of him. She wanted to find out how he'd cut his cheek but she would get that information out of him later.

Having hung up his coat he sat down at his desk and contemplated the pile of letters in his tray without enthusiasm. Angela Blackwood's was on top. She was as prolix in her correspondence as in her novels. He had reached the third typewritten page when the internal phone buzzed. He frowned at it but did not answer. A minute later Mollie opened the door.

'Excuse me. There's a gentleman on the phone. He won't give his name but he insists on speaking to you.'

'Find out what he wants.'

'I've asked him. He won't tell me. But he's very polite,' she added dreamily. 'Got rather a nice voice.'

'Tell him I can't speak to him until I know what it's about,' he answered crossly.

'Yes, all right.'

Mollie retreated, leaving the door ajar. He could faintly hear her voice as he continued to wade through Miss Blackwood's screed. She was back in less than a minute.

'I've spoken to him. He says it's a personal matter— about a *friend* of yours.'

'A friend of mine?' The emphasis on 'friend' struck a chord. 'All right—put him on.'

As she went out, this time closing the door, he put the letter aside and pulled the telephone towards him. When the bell tinkled he picked the receiver up.

'Peter Matty speaking.'

'Mr Matty, I'm sorry to trouble you—if it's an inconvenient time—'

117

As Mollie had said, the voice was a pleasant one. The speaker had the easy manner of someone accustomed to getting his own way.

'Who are you?' Peter interrupted him. 'Who is it speaking?'

'We have a mutual friend,' the caller went on blandly. 'Mrs du Salle. And she's asked me to telephone you and say, first of all, how very sorry she is about the incident which occurred yesterday. And secondly—'

'Look, Mr-whatever-your-name-is,' Peter said, irritated by the man's plausible familiarity, 'if Mrs du Salle has a message for me I'd like her to deliver it personally.'

'Do you know, I thought you'd say that. And I must confess it's a point of view with which I have the utmost sympathy. If you hold on, Mr Matty, I'll see what I can do for you.'

The unexpected change of tactic disconcerted Peter. As the silence on the other end of the line lengthened he began to regret treating the stranger with such brusqueness. Then he heard a low voice which made his heart quicken.

'Peter—it's Phyllis.'

'Where are you? Where are you speaking from—and who was that on the phone just now?' In spite of himself he was firing questions at her, just as he had done in the taxi.

'Peter, please listen to me.' She spoke calmly, absolutely without emotion. 'I'm sorry about yesterday. I lost my head. I shouldn't have disappeared like that.'

'You seem to make a habit of it.'

'I made a mistake in the first place, in letting you drive me down to Dorset that day. I've regretted it ever since. I apologise for all the trouble I've caused you.'

'Look—we can't talk on the phone.' He forced himself

118

to stay calm and keep his voice level. 'I've got to see you. I've a hundred and one questions I want to ask you.'

'I'm sorry,' she answered in the same flat tone. He even wondered if she was speaking under constraint. 'I can't see you. It's quite out of the question.'

'Why is it out of the question?'

'I've just told you. I made a mistake and—I don't want to see you again. I'm sorry, but that's the way it is.'

The unemotional, clinical statement was as hurtful as the blow on the face from the taxi driver.

'Is that really what you want?'

'Yes. I don't want to sound offensive, but there's just no point in our meeting again. I should only regret it.'

'Have I offended you? Have I annoyed you in any way?'

'I just don't want to see you again. It's as simple as that.'

'Yes, well it's not as simple as that so far as I'm concerned.' His sense of hurt replaced by anger, Peter did not care if his voice rose. '*I* want to see *you*. I want to know why you lied to me. Why you told me that story about Sir Arnold Wyatt. Why you deliberately—'

He broke off, holding the receiver away from his ear. The maddening buzz of the dialling tone told him that he had again lost contact with Phyllis du Salle. He listened to it for a long time, as if by some miracle her voice might come back on the line. When he finally put the receiver down it was with a conviction that he would never see her again.

10

'I'll have another one, Don.'

The barman, who was in shirtsleeves and waistcoat, put down the glass he was polishing. He gave his customer a doubtful look.

'A small Scotch, sir,' he suggested.

'No. The same again. A double.'

'Yes, sir,' Don said, but he did not immediately refill the glass.

'Is that—is that three I've had?' Peter's speech was becoming slurred.

'Four, sir.'

'Four? Are you sure?'

'Yes, Mr Matty. Four doubles.'

The Blue Boar was only a couple of hundred yards from Peter's office. It had a friendly and welcoming atmosphere and he had made a habit of dropping in there after office hours. At half past six on this week-day evening the saloon bar was virtually deserted. Apart from Peter there was only one other customer. He too was sitting at one of the high stools in front of the bar. Peter had taken little notice of him, merely noting that he was wearing a check jacket.

Mr Matty was one of Don's most respected regulars. He had never seen him drinking like this before and he was worried.

'Are you sure you'd like another one, sir?'

Peter nodded four times. 'I'm positive.'

'It's none of my business, Mr Matty, but—are you driving, sir?'

'No, I'm not driving. And you're quite right.' Peter prodded a finger at him to emphasise each word. 'It is none of your business.'

'I'm sorry, sir.' Don shrugged and turned away to refill the glass from the row of bottles behind him.

'That's all right.' Peter realised that he was antagonising an old friend. 'No hard feelings. Perhaps you'll join me?'

'That's very kind of you, sir, but not at the moment.'

Don put the glass in front of Peter and slid the water jug towards him. Peter ignored the hint and took a sip of the neat whisky. He fumbled for a cigarette and made several attempts to light it. Without comment Don took his own lighter from his waistcoat pocket and held the flame for Peter.

'Are you a married man, Don?'

'Yes, sir. I'm afraid I am.'

'Don't be afraid. I'm glad to hear it.' Peter held up his glass and his face became comically serious. 'Because this is what happens to a bachelor when he makes a bloody fool of himself.'

'Well—not to worry, sir.' Don glanced at the other customer and winked. 'It happens to all of us, at one time or another.'

The telephone on the shelf behind the barman began to ring.

'Excuse me.' Don picked the receiver up. 'Hello? . . . Yes, it is . . . Who did you say? . . . Yes, he's right here.' He turned to the man in the check coat. 'It's for you, sir.'

'Oh.' He unhooked his heels from the stool and stood up. 'Is there a box?'

'No, I'm sorry. I'm afraid you'll have to take it here, sir.'

'Thank you.'

Don lifted the entire instrument, which was connected by an extendable cord and put it on the bar counter. Peter saw now that the other man was quite tall. His erect bearing suggested that he might have been an army officer. He was in his early forties and had a neatly trimmed moustache. He partly turned his back on Peter and Don as he picked up the receiver.

'Hello? . . . Oh, hello! . . . Where are you, where are you speaking from?' There was a long pause during which Peter and Don avoided each other's eyes and pretended they were not listening. The man's voice was educated and pleasant. Peter was sure he had heard it before but after five double whiskies his memory was vague. 'Are you sure? Are you sure it's our friend? . . . You recognised him? . . . Is he still in the flat? . . . I see . . . No, don't do that, stick to our arrangement. I'll meet you in about fifteen minutes.'

He replaced the receiver and pushed the telephone back across the bar counter. Don returned it to its shelf.

'How much do I owe you?'

'Let me see—that'll be exactly 90p, sir.'

The man in the check coat handed Don a pound. 'Keep the change. Good night.'

He picked up his hat and coat from the back of a chair and put them on. As he moved towards the door he had to pass Peter. He paused and said conversationally: 'I shouldn't stay here too long, Mr Matty. I'm afraid you have rather a busy evening ahead of you.'

Peter stared with eyes that had difficulty in focussing at the back of the tall man as he pushed his way out through the swing doors.

'Who the hell does he think he is? I was just going home in any case.'

He was buttoning up his coat and heading for the door when Don reminded him, 'You haven't paid for your drinks, Mr Matty.'

'Oh, haven't I? How much does it come to?'

'Four pounds twenty, please, sir.'

Peter winced and felt for his wallet. The fresh air hit him as soon as he was outside and he began to wish he had heeded Don's warning. He had to walk a couple of hundred yards before a cruising taxi responded to his wave and picked him up. He slumped gratefully into the seat.

'You be all right, sir?' the driver asked him anxiously when he deposited him at the Royal Hospital end of Sloane Court.

'Yes, quite all right. How much do I owe you?'

It took Peter some time to extract a note from his wallet and count out the necessary change. He realised that he had been over-generous when the driver thanked him warmly. He was still standing on the edge of the pavement when the driver pulled out from the kerb. There was a screech of tyres as a red Triumph Spitfire, travelling far too fast, swerved round the front of the taxi, missing it by inches. The car's hood was down and Peter could see the back of the driver's head as he disappeared round the next corner.

At the entrance to the flats he was fumbling for his keys before he remembered that the main door was not locked till after dark. He was talking to himself as he approached the door of his own flat. He got the key in the lock at the third attempt. He hung his coat up in the hall and went into the sitting room.

Then he stopped dead. The shock of the scene which confronted him sobered him up as quickly as a bucket of cold water sluiced over his head. The room was a shambles. The bookshelves had been stripped, the books flung in piles on the floor. His desk had been ransacked, every drawer taken out and the contents dumped on the carpet. The cupboard had received the same treatment. The cabinet where he kept his supply of drinks had been forced open. A bottle of gin had been broken and was dripping its contents through the shelf. There was no corner of the room that had been left untouched. Even the pictures had been wrenched from the walls to make sure that nothing was concealed behind them.

Appalled and sickened, he went through to his bedroom, only to be met by the same spectacle of ruthless devastation.

The Victorian pub in Islington was open for business. As he passed the door Peter could hear Henry Higgins screaming his head off to the accompaniment of grotesquely amplified electric guitars. This time there were no kids playing football at the entrance to the flats where Max lived. The lift was still out of order. The long climb up the stairs did nothing to improve Peter's temper. The sense of injury and defilement which he had felt on first seeing his ransacked flat had turned to a cold anger, fuelled by the whisky in him.

He gave a sharp rap on Max's door with the ornamental knocker. He thought he heard a scuffle of movement inside, but no one came to answer his summons. He knocked again and rang the bell, keeping his finger on the button for at least ten seconds.

Several minutes passed and he'd knocked and rung repeatedly before he heard Max's voice from inside the door. He sounded angry.

'Who is it?'

'It's Peter. Peter Matty. I want to talk to you.'

There was silence from the other side. He was beginning to think that Max would refuse to see him when the key was turned in the lock and the door opened. Max was wearing a silk dressing-gown and apparently little else. His feet were bare and his hair was tousled. There were smudges of lipstick on his face.

'Hello, Peter. What the hell are you doing here?'

Peter pushed past him and strode straight into the lounge. The room was empty but cigarette smoke hung in the air and there was a smell of cheap perfume. A pair of men's gloves lay on the settee where they had been thrown.

Max, with an aggrieved expression, had followed Peter through the hall. Peter swung round to face him.

'Did you go to my flat this evening?'

'Your flat?'

'Yes.'

'No. Why? You look devilishly agitated, Squire. What is it?'

'If you didn't go to my flat what were you doing in Royal Hospital Road?'

'In Royal Hospital Road?' Max repeated, puzzled.

'Yes.'

'When was I in Royal Hospital Road?'

'About half an hour ago. You were in your car. I saw you.'

Max shook his head emphatically. 'Not me! I've been here the whole afternoon. I took a friend out to lunch and we've—' With a grin Max nodded towards the closed door of his bedroom. 'We've been here ever since. But what the devil is this all about? Why the excitement?'

Max's protestations were so convincing that Peter began to have doubts. Yet he had been sure that the man he had glimpsed at the wheel of the sports car had been Max. And Max drove a red Triumph Spitfire.

Still watching his face closely he said: 'Someone broke into my flat. They ransacked the place, searched it from top to bottom.'

'Jeez! I'm sorry to hear that.' Max's expressive face showed deep concern. 'That's awful, Squire. But I still fail to see what it's got to do with—'

He broke off, his concern giving way to injured innocence.

'Good God! You surely don't think I was responsible?'

'Were you?' Peter demanded bluntly.

'You must be out of your tiny mind!' Max for once showed real annoyance. 'I've just told you. I've been here the whole afternoon.'

His head turned as he saw something over Peter's shoulder. Peter spun round. The bedroom door had opened and a girl had come out. She was plump and sexy. Her hair was in disarray. The lipstick on her mouth was smeared. She was holding one of Max's coat-style shirts round her. It was unbuttoned and did little to conceal her curves. Her expression was petulant.

'What's going on, Max?'

Max didn't answer her. He turned back to face Peter.

'Now do you believe me?'

126

The saloon bar of the Blue Boar was well filled by the time Peter returned. Most of the tables round the edge of the room were occupied and all the stools at the bar were taken. Don was hard put to it to deal with all the demands of his customers. Peter had to wait for three other people to be served. Don seemed reluctant to catch his eye.

'Hey, Don!' Peter called as he saw him start to move to the other end of the counter.

'Oh, Mr Matty!' Don pretended that he had not noticed him before. 'I didn't expect to see you again this evening.'

'No, I don't suppose you did.'

'What would you like, sir?'

'I'd like a large Scotch but I'll settle for a tomato juice.'

'Certainly, sir,' Don said, relieved. He could see that Peter had sobered up remarkably since his earlier visit.

'Don.' Peter called him back as he was going to get the tomato juice. He kept his voice low as he asked: 'You remember the man in the check sports jacket who was sitting over there earlier this evening? He spoke to me just as he was leaving.'

'Yes. Mr Talmadge.'

'Talmadge. Is that his name?'

'Yes, sir.'

'Who is he, Don?'

'Well—' Don sucked his cheeks in. 'I'm not really sure who he is. I believe he's something to do with the Arts Council, but I'm not sure.'

'Is he one of your regulars?'

'No, I wouldn't say that. Although he's certainly been in here quite a few times during the past few weeks. Funny you should be interested in Mr Talmadge. One lunch time, about a week ago, you were having a drink with a friend of yours. Mr Lerner, I think his name is.'

'Yes. That's right. Max Lerner.'

'Well, after you'd gone Mr Talmadge started asking me questions about him. Just coming, sir.'

This last remark was to a customer who was signalling with a pound note to catch Don's attention.

'What sort of questions, Don?'

Don grinned. 'The sort you're asking me now. Who is he? What does he do? Is he one of your regulars?'

'Were you able to satisfy his curiosity?'

'I told him Mr Lerner was a journalist and the only thing I knew about him was that he had alimony trouble.'

'I see.' Peter watched Don fetch a bottle of tomato juice, prise the cap off and pour it into a small glass. 'Did Mr Talmadge question you about me, by any chance?'

'No, he didn't. It was your friend he was interested in. Would you like Worcester sauce in the tomato juice, sir?'

'It seems to me, Peter, that you've got to make up your mind where you go from here.' Claude and Peter were facing each other across the table in the cabin of *First Edition*. Peter had driven down from London earlier that evening, arriving in time to share supper with his brother. Now they were sitting over a cup of coffee, and each of them had a glass of brandy in front of him. 'Either you're going to let yourself become further and further involved in this business or—'

'It isn't a question of my *wanting* to get further involved.'

'I don't agree.'

'But, Claude, just look what's happened during the past week. My flat was ransacked. I was damn nearly arrested. Max Lerner suddenly changed his mind about—'

128

'Peter, listen,' Claude cut in. 'Please listen to me, there's a good chap.' He finished his coffee and put his elbows on the table. 'I can't account for what happened during the past week. I don't know why your flat was ransacked. I don't know why Mortimer Brown switched the photographs—if he did switch them—and I haven't the slightest idea who this chap Talmadge is. But one thing I do know. None of these things would have happened to you if you hadn't tried to get friendly with Phyllis du Salle.' He saw that Peter was about to protest and held up his hand. 'Peter, please. Whether you like it or not you've got to make your mind up. Either you forget this girl, put her completely out of your mind, or you take the consequences. And God only knows what they might turn out to be.'

Peter was lighting up yet another cigarette. The ashtray already contained half a dozen stubs.

'I'm sorry, Claude. I can't put her out of my mind. I've tried. It's just—no use. I've got to find her and I've got to talk to her.'

'But Peter,' Claude pointed out patiently, 'you *have* talked to her. You talked to her on the telephone and she didn't want to have anything more to do with you.'

'I don't think she was telling the truth.'

'That's not what you said a few minutes ago when I questioned you about the call. You said she sounded distinctly unfriendly.'

'I think she may have been forced to speak as she did.'

Peter was at his most obstinate. His infatuation over Phyllis du Salle—for that was what Claude believed it to be—had warped his judgement to such an extent that he could not think logically any more. He badly needed fatherly advice. Claude decided to have one more try.

'Look, Peter—you asked me for my opinion and I'm giving it to you. If you continue with this affair, if you insist on—'

He broke off, listening. There had been a step on the deck overhead.

'Mr Matty,' a familiar voice called. 'It's Mrs Frinton.'

'Come along down, Mrs Frinton,' Peter invited.

Mrs Frinton came gingerly down the steps into the cabin.

'Sorry to disturb you,' she looked from Claude to Peter, 'but there's been a phone message for you from a Mrs Cassidy.'

'Sir Arnold Wyatt's housekeeper,' Peter reminded Claude. 'What did she say, Mrs Frinton?'

'She said she'd like you to meet her tomorrow morning, if possible. She'll be at Fletcher's Café in Heatherdown about eleven o'clock.'

'Is that all she said?'

'No, she said she wanted to explain about the photograph.'

'The photograph?'

'That's what she said, dearie.'

'Thank you, Mrs Frinton.' As she turned to go Peter remembered his good manners. 'Oh—would you like a cup of coffee, or a drink perhaps?'

'No, thank you. That's very kind of you, but I must get back. I'm trying to do my accounts and—oh, dear!' She chuckled at her own human frailty. 'I'm in a frightful muddle, I'm afraid.'

By the middle of the morning a lot of cars had come into Heatherdown. Peter decided to leave the Jaguar in the official park. His meeting with Mrs Cassidy might turn out to be a long one. He put the necessary coins in the ticket dispenser and stuck the ticket on the inside of his windscreen.

He had a couple of hundred yards to walk before reaching Fletcher's Café, where he and Claude had taken coffee that morning when he had seen Phyllis du Salle's photograph in Mortimer Brown's window. His route now took him through the High Street and past the photographer's shop.

As he turned into Heatherdown's main thoroughfare he found that the traffic had slowed to a crawl because of some hold-up further on. Looking ahead he saw that the street was partly blocked by an ambulance and a couple of hastily parked police cars. Blue lights were flashing on all three vehicles. A crowd had collected on the pavement and was spilling out over the road. It all seemed to be happening right outside Mortimer Brown's shop.

He quickened his pace and as he drew nearer he saw that uniformed police were keeping the onlookers back from the semi-circular space round the police cars and ambulance. Two men in plain clothes were standing on the steps of the shop, deep in serious conversation. They had an efficient and observant air which stamped them as CID officers.

Peter pushed his way through to the front of the crowd in time to see the two ambulancemen emerge from the shop carrying a stretcher. The body lying on it was completely covered by a blanket. In a leisurely manner which made it clear that the casualty was past human aid they began to load it into their vehicle.

'What's happened, do you know?' Peter asked an oldish fellow who was carrying his wife's shopping bag.

'There's been a murder,' the man answered with relish.

'Murder?'

'Ay,' his wife confirmed. 'It's the chap what owns the place, the photographer.'

'Mortimer Brown?' Peter was staggered by the statement. 'Mortimer Brown's been murdered?'

The woman nodded. 'Yes, I think so.'

Peter stared at the body. The photographer had been strangely shrunken by death. The ambulancemen pushed the stretcher forward on its runners and closed the doors. The police opened up a passage through the crowd so that it could move away.

Peter saw the younger and probably more junior of the two CID men start towards one of the police cars. He walked forward to intercept him. The detective-sergeant paused as he saw this young man coming out of the crowd with such self-confidence and authority.

'Excuse me, officer.'

The sergeant looked at him, sizing him up. This could be a reporter representing one of the big London papers.

'Can you tell me what's happened?'

'There's been a murder, sir,' the sergeant replied, a little coldly.

'Yes, I know. But what happened exactly? How was he murdered?'

'He?'

'Mr Brown?'

'I'm afraid you've been misinformed, sir.' The sergeant put a hand on the door of the car. He pointed towards the shop. 'That's Mr Brown standing over there.'

As the sergeant got into the car Peter looked in the direction he had pointed. Mortimer Brown had emerged and was in conversation with the other CID man. His face was pale and he was talking excitedly, making exaggerated gestures with his hands.

The police driver had started his engine, but the window on the sergeant's side was still lowered. Peter stooped to ask him.

'Who's been murdered, then?'

'A woman, sir. A Mrs Cassidy.'

11

'Mrs Cassidy?'

The CID man saw that Peter was shocked by his announcement. It was evident that the name meant something to him.

'What—how did it happen?'

'Are you a reporter, sir?'

'No.' Peter was still staring towards the shop. 'But I knew Mrs Cassidy slightly. I had an appointment with her this morning.'

'This morning?'

'Yes. At eleven o'clock.'

The sergeant opened the door of the car again and got out.

'Tell me about this appointment, sir.'

'I was supposed to meet her in the café, the one across the road. She telephoned a friend of mine last night and—' Peter stopped and turned to the sergeant. 'You still haven't answered my question. How was she murdered?'

'She was shot. She'd just entered the photographer's when, according to Mr Brown, a car raced by and someone fired several shots. Mrs Cassidy was hit.'

'When did this happen?'

'About twenty minutes ago.'

'Were the shots intended for Mrs Cassidy?'

'That's a good question, sir. We're not sure.'

He was looking towards the photographer's shop. His inspector had finished his conversation. Mortimer Brown had gone back into the shop. The inspector was walking over to rejoin his colleague.

'This gentleman had an appointment with Mrs Cassidy,' he explained when the inspector arrived.

'Indeed?'

The inspector gazed at Peter with interest. He was in his mid-thirties, with a broad moustache and sharp brown eyes set rather close together.

'They were supposed to meet in Fletcher's,' the sergeant added.

'Was Mrs Cassidy a friend of yours, sir?'

'No. She worked for Sir Arnold Wyatt. She was his housekeeper.'

'Yes, we know that,' the inspector said impatiently. 'But was she a friend of yours?'

'No, she wasn't, but she telephoned me last night and said she wanted to see me.' The inspector had raised his eyebrows. His steady stare was disconcerting. 'My name is Matty. Peter Matty. I'm a publisher. I live in London but I've got a boat down here, or rather in Poole Harbour. Several weeks ago I had occasion to visit Sir Arnold Wyatt and Mrs Cassidy happened to be—' A number of inquisitive onlookers, seeing a stranger apparently being questioned by the police, had crowded round and were listening to the exchange. 'Look, I'm sorry, this is impossible. We can't talk here.'

'I agree, Mr Matty,' the inspector said. 'Let's go down to the station. Have you a car?'

'Yes.'

'Then perhaps you'd get your car and follow us, sir.'

'Er—yes, all right. I'll get it. It's in the car park.'

As Peter moved away up the High Street Inspector Lane and Detective-Sergeant Colford watched him thoughtfully.

'Peter Matty,' Colford said. 'Have you heard of him?'
'I'm not sure. I seem to know the name.'

Sir Arnold Wyatt returned from London on the afternoon train. He was enough of a traditionalist to consider that a gentleman going up to Town should be properly dressed. He wore a homburg hat, a black overcoat with velvet collar, a pinstripe dark grey suit and a pair of venerable Lobb shoes. The leather briefcase in his hand dated from his early days as a lawyer. His taxi was waiting for him as he came out of the station.

As the car came up the drive of Forest Gate Manor he was looking forward to the tea and muffins which Mrs Cassidy would have waiting for him. When it turned the last bend before the house he saw the police car parked outside the front door. The driver was still in his seat. Two men in plain clothes were just moving away from the house. They stopped when they saw the taxi.

Sensing trouble, Wyatt got out warily. The older of the two plain-clothes men approached him.

'Sir Arnold Wyatt?'

'Yes.'

'I'm Detective-Inspector Lane, sir.'

'Yes, I know. I recognised you. What is it? Has something happened? Don't tell me my house has been broken into!'

'No, sir.' Lane's face was serious. 'It's your housekeeper. Mrs Cassidy. I'm afraid—she's dead, sir.'

'I know exactly how you feel, sir, and believe me I have no wish to make a nuisance of myself, but I'd be very grateful if you could answer one or two questions.'

Wyatt had paid off his taxi and invited the two CID men

136

into the house. Fortunately he always carried a key to his front door on the ring attached to his braces button. He was sitting on the settee in his study, a tumbler of whisky in his hand. The two detectives had refused a drink. They were sitting on the easy chairs, not lounging back but alert and upright. Their manner was formal as they waited for Wyatt to recover from the shock. Lane was facing him and Colford was placed so that he could watch his profile—and his hands.

'Yes. Yes, of course.' Wyatt made an effort to pull himself together. 'I'm sorry, Inspector. It was such a shock. But tell me, please. What happened? You say she was shot?'

'Yes,' Lane said. 'Mrs Cassidy had just entered the shop—Mortimer Brown's. A shot was fired—presumably from the street, but we're not sure—and Mrs Cassidy was hit. She died almost immediately.'

'But why on earth should anyone want to kill my house-keeper? It just doesn't make sense.'

Lane did not answer the question. He waited a moment before asking, 'When did you last see Mrs Cassidy, sir?'

'This morning. I left the house about eight o'clock. I took my little grand-daughter up to London. She's staying the weekend with some friends of mine.'

'You caught the eight-forty-five?'

Wyatt finished his whisky and put the tumbler down on the coffee table.

'Yes, that's right. Well—in theory the eight-forty-five. It was nearly ten past nine when we left Heatherdown.'

'And you left Mrs Cassidy here, in the house? Was she alone?'

'Yes.' Wyatt nodded. The familiar pattern of question and answer was steadying him.

'Did Mrs Cassidy tell you that she would be going into the village later in the morning?'

'Yes, I think she said she was going to do some shopping.'

'Did she mention that she would be calling at Mortimer Brown's?'

'No, she didn't.'

'Why did she call on Mr Brown, sir—have you any idea?'

'No, I'm afraid I haven't,' Wyatt answered with some of his old vehemence. 'I should ask Mr Brown.'

'We have done so, sir. He doesn't know why she wanted to see her.'

'Neither do I, Inspector.'

Colford, watching Wyatt, was sure that the former barrister's shock and distress had not been counterfeit. The hand toying with the empty tumbler had become steadier under questioning.

'Just one more question, sir, then we'll leave you in peace. Did you know that Mrs Cassidy had an appointment this morning with a man called Peter Matty?'

'No, I didn't.' Surprised, Wyatt turned round and found Colford's deadpan eyes fixed on him.

'You know Mr Matty, sir?' Lane said.

'Yes, I do. He's a publisher. He called round to see me about— But what makes you think Mrs Cassidy had an appointment with him?'

'According to Mr Matty, your housekeeper telephoned him last night and asked to see him. They arranged to meet this morning in Heatherdown.'

'Well—this is news to me, Inspector!' Wyatt said emphatically. 'I certainly knew nothing about any such appointment.'

Lane gave Colford an almost imperceptible nod. Both men got to their feet.

'Thank you for your co-operation, sir. We will keep in touch with you.'

Peter slowed from seventy miles per hour to forty as he approached the speed-limit sign on the outskirts of Heatherdown. He dipped his headlights for a motor cyclist coming out of the town, and kept them lowered. The sodium lamps in the High Street gave a sinister but effective illumination.

'I do appreciate what you're doing, Claude.'

'So you should,' Claude said drily, 'because I'm dead against it.'

'Claude, it's no use, I've just got to find out what the hell this is all about. I've got to find out why Mrs Cassidy wanted to talk to me.'

'Well, you know my views on all this. I don't have to reiterate them.'

'You think I should call it a day and forget what happened this morning?'

'Yes, I do.'

Peter glanced in his driving mirror. There was a pair of headlights following him. He reduced his speed to the legal thirty mph.

'You don't sound very convincing.'

'Peter, I understand how you feel and if I were in your shoes I should probably feel the same. But I'm worried. I like it less and less.'

'What is it you don't like?'

'Well, apart from your flat being searched, I don't like the fact that shortly after she contacted you Mrs Cassidy was murdered.'

'In other words, you think something unpleasant could very easily happen to me?'

'If you continue to let yourself be drawn into this affair—yes, I do.'

'Yes, well, if you don't want to go ahead with this just say so.' Peter braked and began to pull in towards the kerb. They were passing Mortimer Brown's shop and the bridge was just ahead. 'There'll be no hard feelings, I assure you.'

'No, no, I'll go ahead with it.'

'Sir Arnold's far more likely to confide in you, Claude. I'm sure of that.'

'If he has anything to confide. You want me to try and find out whether he knew about your appointment with Mrs Cassidy?'

The car following had gone past. Peter picked up speed again.

'And if he did know, then what was it all about?'

Claude brandished the LP he was holding on his lap. It was one of his own recordings which had just been released.

'Well—we'll see what we can do.'

The curtains had not been drawn over the windows of Forest Gate Manor. It was symbolic of Sir Arnold Wyatt's dependence on his housekeeper for the proper running of his house. The light from the study could be seen shining out over the lawn.

Peter dropped Claude outside the front door.

'I'll be waiting for you in that little lane by the gate.'

Claude waited till the Jaguar's tail lights had disappeared down the drive before he rang the bell. He had the parcel containing the LP in his hand. Almost at once he heard footsteps in the hall. Wyatt himself opened the door. Judging by the alacrity with which he had answered the bell he had been expecting a visitor. He was obviously surprised to see Claude standing there.

'Good evening, Sir Arnold.'

Wyatt recovered himself. 'Why—hello, Mr Matty.'

'I hope I'm not disturbing you.'

'No. No, not at all.'

'Could you spare me a few moments?'

'Yes, of course.' Wyatt glanced down the drive. 'Did you walk up?'

'My brother dropped me. He has some business to attend to in Heatherdown.'

'Please come in.'

Claude walked into the hall.

'Do forgive me,' Wyatt said as he closed the door. 'I was expecting someone else and I did not immediately recognise you.'

'I thought you might like this.' Claude handed him the parcel. 'It's a new recording of mine, the one I mentioned. I received copies this morning.'

A smile of pleasure lit Wyatt's harassed face. 'How very thoughtful of you! This really is most kind. Come into the drawing room, Mr Matty.'

He opened the door of a room nearer the front door than the study and switched on the central chandelier. It was beautifully furnished with period pieces. The room had none of the companionable untidiness of the study.

Wyatt crossed the room to switch on an electric fire.

'Can I offer you a drink?'

'No, I don't think so, thank you.'

'It's curious you should call. I intended to get in touch with you, or rather your brother, first thing tomorrow morning.'

'About Mrs Cassidy.'

'Yes.' Wyatt took the LP from its wrapping, looked at the sleeve. He nodded, and put it down on the arm of the sofa.

'My brother was in Heatherdown this morning shortly after she was shot.'

'Yes—the police told me.'

'It must have been a terrible shock to you. When I heard the news I was appalled, I couldn't believe it.'

'Yes, I know. I know—' Wyatt stared blankly through the window at the darkness outside. He shook his head despairingly. 'Even now I just can't believe it's happened. I was in London. I knew nothing about it, absolutely nothing, until I arrived home.'

'Have the police any idea who did it?'

'I don't think so. If they have they certainly did not confide in me. It's utterly and completely beyond my comprehension why anyone should want to kill my house-keeper.' Wyatt suddenly realised he was keeping his guest standing. 'But please, do sit down.'

Claude considered the available options and chose a wing chair with a high back.

'Are you sure I can't offer you a drink?'

'Yes, I'm sure, thank you.'

'How's your brother, Mr Matty?' Wyatt asked. It was clear that the inquiry was prompted by politeness rather than any real concern for Peter's health. 'He's well, I trust?'

'Yes, he is, but I'm afraid he's very bewildered at the moment, and very upset. He had an appointment to see Mrs Cassidy. That's why he was in Heatherdown.'

Wyatt at last ceased his agitated prowling and sat down on the settee facing Claude.

'Yes, I know.'

'You knew about the appointment?' Claude asked, surprised.

'The Inspector told me about it, and I must confess it

was news to me. I didn't realise that your brother and Mrs Cassidy were acquainted.'

'I don't think they were—except for his visits here.'

'Then who made the appointment?'

'Mrs Cassidy did. She telephoned Peter, or rather left a message for him, asking him to meet her in Fletcher's Café.'

'Now why on earth should she do that?'

'She said she wanted to explain about the photograph. I can only assume that she meant the photograph of your daughter, the one that was in Brown's window. The one my brother mistook for Phyllis du Salle.'

'I find this very odd.' Wyatt's fingers, seeking something to toy with, found one of the ornamental tassels on the sofa. 'Was this the first time Mrs Cassidy had contacted your brother?'

'So far as I know.' Claude paused before asking the question to which Peter wanted an answer. 'Sir Arnold, forgive my asking, but did you discuss my brother with your housekeeper? Did you tell her what happened the morning we went to Mortimer Brown's?'

'Yes, I did,' Wyatt answered without hesitation.

'And what was her reaction?'

'She thought your brother was imagining things. She thought he'd become so obsessed by this Mrs du Salle that he was—well—' Wyatt gave a half smile and shrugged.

'Unbalanced?'

'Yes.'

'Is that what you think?'

'I just don't know what to think.' Again Wyatt's gaze strayed to the darkness beyond the window. He gave the impression that he was listening for some sound from outside. 'I'm so bewildered by the turn of events and by

143

what happened to Mrs Cassidy that—' His eyes came back to Claude. 'Mr Matty, I shouldn't tell you this. I promised not to. I promised not to say a word to anyone, but I feel I must confide in you.' He leant forward, clasping his fingers. 'Twenty-four hours before I first met your brother a man called Talmadge telephoned me. He said he wanted to see me, urgently. When I asked him what it was he wanted to see me about he said: "I want to talk to you about a very old friend of yours, Sir Arnold—Norman du Salle."'

'Norman du Salle? Was du Salle a friend of yours?'

'Yes, he was.'

'But that's not what you told Peter,' said Claude angrily. 'You told Peter you'd never heard of him.'

'Yes—yes, I know what I told your brother, Mr Matty.' Wyatt bit on his lower lip in his discomfiture. 'But please listen to me. Listen to what I've got to say—'

Julian Talmadge knew he was half an hour late for his appointment as he drove up the avenue of Forest Gate Manor. He took a briefcase from the back seat of the Rover before he got out and went to ring the door bell. For good measure he also gave a sharp and authoritative rat-tat with the knocker. When there was no response he frowned and went through the process again. Talmadge was not accustomed to being kept waiting.

When at last Wyatt opened the door he was apologetic and a little flustered.

'Sorry to have kept you waiting.'

'Good evening, Sir Arnold. I'm a little late.' Ostentatiously he looked at his watch. 'I think I said eight o'clock.'

'Yes, I—er—was expecting you earlier. Come in.' Talmadge scrutinised him sharply before entering the hall. 'Let me take your coat.'

'Thank you.'

The new visitor took off his coat and scarf. He was wearing the same check coat as when Peter had seen him in the Blue Boar. He realised, as Wyatt took his things and put them on a chair, that his host was ill at ease.

'Are you alone?'

'No,' Wyatt admitted. 'I was just going to tell you. I've got a visitor, I'm afraid. He's in the drawing room.'

'That's all right. I can wait.'

'Would you like to go in the study?'

'Will your visitor be long?'

'I don't think so. It's Mr Matty.'

'Peter Matty?'

'No. It's his brother, Claude.'

'You never told me Claude Matty was a friend of yours,' Talmadge said with a hint of accusation.

'You never asked me. In any case he could hardly be called a friend of mine on the strength of—'

'Then what's he doing here?'

'Ostensibly he brought me a present, a gramophone record.' Wyatt was keeping his voice down, though he had closed the drawing room door. 'But I'm afraid it was painfully obvious the record was just an excuse. He wanted to talk about his brother and the—what happened to Mrs Cassidy.'

Talmadge reflected for a minute, gazing down on Wyatt. 'Well, in that case perhaps you'd better introduce me and we'll put him in the picture.' He gave a wintry smile. 'That is, of course, if you haven't already done so.'

Peter had the car radio turned on low and was listening to a concert from the Festival Hall. With the engine switched off the car was cold. He did not want to start the

145

car in case the sound attracted attention. The Jaguar was well concealed behind a hedge at the bottom of Sir Arnold Wyatt's drive in a little lane that no one was likely to use at night. Nothing and nobody had passed except a car which had gone up the drive to the Manor. A shower of rain had passed and drops were plopping on the Jaguar from the branches of the tree above him.

He was stubbing out his fifth cigarette when he saw a dim figure outlined against the road outside the gates. As it came towards him he recognised Claude. He opened his door and stepped out to meet him.

'You've been a devil of a time.'

'Yes, I know.'

'I was getting quite worried. Did you see Wyatt?'

'Yes, I did. And not only Wyatt. Peter, let's get in the car.'

Peter grabbed his arm. 'What do you mean—not only Wyatt? Who else did you see? Who was in that car?'

'I saw the man you told me about. The man who spoke to you in the pub.'

'Talmadge?'

'That's right. Julian Talmadge.'

Peter could not see Claude's face in the darkness, but he was sure that his brother was holding back something.

'Is he a friend of Wyatt's?'

'No,' Claude said, still with that evasive manner, 'not exactly.'

'Then what was he doing there?'

Claude tried to move towards the Jaguar, but Peter would not release his hold on his brother's arm.

'Claude, who *is* this man?'

'He's with Scotland Yard. Attached to the Special Branch.'

'Good God!' Peter let his arm fall.

'Get in the car, Peter. We're going back to the house. Talmadge wants to talk to you.'

'All right—I accept who you are, and what you are,' Peter told Talmadge. 'Now get to the point.'

'Which particular point have you got in mind, sir?'

'My brother said you wanted to talk to me.'

During Claude's absence Wyatt had fetched in a tray of drinks and glasses. Claude and Talmadge each had a glass in his hand and Wyatt was pouring himself a whisky. Peter had refused a drink—and a chair. He was standing near the sofa looking down at Talmadge. The latter appeared blissfully unaware of the irritation he was causing Peter. He sat with his legs languidly crossed and a look of faint amusement on his face.

'Yes, I thought perhaps, in the circumstances, that might be a good idea. But I'm beginning to wonder.' He stood up and his languid manner vanished. He topped Peter by a good three inches. 'Mr Matty, I realise that you've been extremely worried just recently, and I must admit, to a certain extent, I've been responsible. But believe me, no one's been trying to make a fool out of you, as you seem to be suggesting. Now be sensible, just relax and listen to what Sir Arnold and I have to tell you.'

'Are you sure you won't have a drink?' Wyatt repeated his invitation nervously.

'Thank you, no.'

Wyatt brought his own drink over from the side table. He perched himself on the arm of one of the chairs. Talmadge gave him a nod to indicate that the floor was his.

'Many years ago I befriended a young man called Norman du Salle,' Wyatt began. 'He was the son of a very dear friend of mine. Norman was an ambitious boy and immediately he was twenty-one he emigrated to America. He made a success over there and for several years wrote a newspaper column which was widely syndicated. Then about seven or eight years ago his work deteriorated somewhat and his column was discontinued. During the course of his career, as you can well imagine, he had met a great many important people. Presidents, prime ministers, ambassadors, famous actors, business tycoons—he met them all. And invariably he gathered information about them. Confidential information, about their private affairs. I regret to say, in recent years, he made use of that information.'

Wyatt paused to take a drink of whisky. He was deriving no pleasure from telling this story.

'You mean blackmail?'

'Yes, Mr Matty. Blackmail. And not only blackmail.' Wyatt glanced at Talmadge, who warned him with a frown not to elucidate this statement. 'About seven years ago a young man named Martin Clifford called on me. He was an American, a freelance journalist, and he had a letter of introduction from Norman—whom, incidentally, I hadn't seen since he emigrated. Martin was a strange young man but since he was a friend of Norman's I invited him to stay with me. He stayed for several weeks and eventually, I regret to say, married my daughter.'

Wyatt glanced at Talmadge as though hoping that the Special Branch man would take up the tale.

'Go on, Sir Arnold,' Talmadge said.

'Although I never liked Martin it was only recently, quite recently, in fact, that I learned the truth about him from Mr Talmadge. I'm ashamed to say it—he worked for Norman.'

The distaste on Wyatt's face was plain. He stood up and took his glass to the window where he stood, looking out into the night. Talmadge realised that he would have to finish the story.

'Unfortunately,' he said, 'du Salle's activities were not confined to the United States. He had an important contact in this country—a man called George Delta. When Mrs du Salle decided to visit England we felt sure that sooner or later Delta would try and get in touch with her. And that, for the record, is when we became interested in you, Mr Matty.'

'In me?'

'Yes.' Talmadge's manner had become almost paternal, as if Peter were a prodigal son who had returned to the fold after a long absence in the haunts of vice.

'But why me?'

'You spoke to Mrs du Salle on the plane. You made a point of getting friendly with her. You tried to take her out to dinner. In short, we thought you were George Delta.'

12

Like most publishers Peter did a great deal of his work away from the office. The constant interruptions to which he was subjected at the headquarters of Matty Books made it impossible to concentrate on any piece of sustained reading. He had brought down to Poole half a dozen manuscripts, or rather typescripts, which had been recommended for publication by his outside readers. All they needed now was his own final assessment and decision. He had spent the morning trying to concentrate on a long novel set in seventeenth-century Scotland. Claude went off to do some shopping at eleven o'clock, leaving him alone on *First Edition*. As midday approached he found it harder and harder to concentrate and kept looking at his watch.

It was five minutes past twelve when he heard the purr of a powerful but well-silenced engine. It stopped somewhere near the boat and he heard a door slam. He put the typescript away and went up the steps onto the deck.

A brilliantly polished black Rover 2600 was standing on the quayside. The official driver was just getting back into his seat, having opened the door for one of the passengers in the rear. It was a slim girl with auburn hair. She was wearing a two-piece skirt-suit, with an open-necked blouse. A silk scarf was tied with studied negligence round her neck. She was standing talking to Julian Talmadge, who was still inside the car.

It was Talmadge who spotted Peter first. He said something to Phyllis. She turned round and for what seemed a long time they looked at each other. Then Peter gave her a wave and a smile. She responded a little shyly. Then, with a final word to Talmadge, she walked towards *First Edition*.

There was considerable restraint between them at first. Phyllis was obviously nervous. Peter knew that she had come down to see him at Talmadge's instigation. He was determined not to make the same mistake as last time and rush her with questions. Sticking carefully to safe subjects like the weather and her drive down from London he plied her with sherry and sat her down at a table under an awning on the deck. It was a clear day and the sun was pleasantly warm.

It was Phyllis herself who brought the conversation round to the subject which was on both their minds.

'Julian Talmadge said that he's told you about Norman—how he was involved in blackmail with a man called Martin Clifford.'

'Sir Arnold's son-in-law. Yes.'

'Believe me, Peter,' she said with great sincerity. 'I never for one moment thought you were involved. I told Talmadge so the very first time we met but he wouldn't believe me. He must have asked me a hundred times what we talked about the day you brought me down here.'

'He thought I worked for your husband, that I was the man they'd been looking for—George Delta.'

'Yes. He told me.'

Peter asked: 'Had you heard of Delta before Talmadge mentioned him?'

'Yes.' She was meeting his eyes with complete frankness.

The sunlight was reflected upwards from the water onto her face. He could tell that she had taken a lot of trouble with her make-up that morning and he regarded that as a favourable sign. 'Linda Braithwaite mentioned his name. We were having a drink together one evening in Geneva and suddenly, quite out of the blue, she asked me if I knew him.'

'Did you tell Talmadge that?'

'I didn't have to tell him.'

'What do you mean?'

'Linda worked for Talmadge. That's why she got friendly with me in Switzerland, and followed me to London. I had certain letters and tape recordings which belonged to Norman and they thought—They were frightened I was going to hand them over to you, or rather to George Delta.'

'I see.' Peter tossed his cigarette end over the side. A cruising seagull, mistaking it for fodder, swooped and picked it out of the water. 'You know what happened to Mrs Braithwaite?'

'Yes, I know.' Phyllis's mouth trembled. 'I was actually staying with her the day she was murdered. She'd been to a meeting at Scotland Yard and was on her way home when George Delta picked her up. At least, that's the theory.'

'You say you were staying with her?'

'Yes. It was Talmadge's idea that I went into hiding. He was worried about my safety. He said that until they'd identified Delta my life was in danger. He was very persuasive, Peter! I really had no alternative.'

Peter realised that he had been staring at her too intently. She had mistaken his concentration for incredulity. He lit another cigarette and asked his next question more casually.

'When did you first meet Talmadge?'

'The day I came down here with you and you persuaded me to borrow your car. You remember I'd spoken to Sir Arnold on the phone and he'd invited me to spend the weekend with him.'

'I remember very well,' Peter said with a smile. 'I've been wondering ever since what happened to you that evening.'

'It's quite an extraordinary story, Peter. I'm not sure that you'll believe me.'

'Try me.'

Phyllis gazed across the blue water towards Brownsea Island. Half a dozen yachts were out in the lagoon, tacking to and fro.

'When I drove up to Forest Gate Manor that evening,' she began, 'there was a police car parked outside the door. The driver was still sitting in it. I thought it was funny the way he watched me as I got out of my car. He gave me the impression that he'd been waiting for *me*. I didn't take any notice of him, just took my suitcase out of the Jaguar. I was going to the front door when I heard him get out of his car. He came over, gave me a friendly sort of salute. "Mrs du Salle?" he said. I was surprised that he knew my name, even more surprised when he insisted on taking my suitcase.'

'Was he in uniform?' Peter asked.

'Yes. He was very polite, asked me how far I'd come, had I had a good drive—that sort of thing. It was he who rang the door bell and when Mrs Cassidy opened it he said, "Would you tell Sir Arnold that Mrs du Salle has arrived?" Mrs Cassidy offered to take my case but this policeman insisted on bringing it in.'

She glanced at him and saw that she had his fullest attention.

'Mrs Cassidy took me to the study and showed me in. I was absolutely amazed! Linda Braithwaite was standing at the far end of the room talking to an important-looking man in police uniform. Sir Arnold was by the fireplace with a very tall man. For some reason I thought he must be a soldier.'

'Talmadge?' Peter suggested.

She nodded. 'They all stopped talking the moment I appeared. It was a horrid moment, Peter! Then Sir Arnold stepped forward and rescued me. "Mrs du Salle, I'm Sir Arnold Wyatt."'

Phyllis broke off, smiling. She had given quite a good imitation of Wyatt.

'You know the rather pompous way he talks, Peter. "I'm Sir Arnold Wyatt. May I introduce you to Chief-Superintendent Mannering and Mr Julian Talmadge. Mrs Braithwaite I think you've already met."'

Peter laughed at her parody, but she quickly became serious again.

'Of course I was wondering most of all about Linda Braithwaite. It must have been two or three minutes before I realised that Talmadge was talking to me about my husband. And then gradually, it dawned on me, Peter, that at long last I was learning the truth about Norman. It had to be the truth because it explained so many things.'

'What sort of things?'

'When Norman lost his job he was desperately worried about money. And then suddenly the whole situation changed. He literally had money to burn. When I questioned him about this he told me that he had been asked to write a series of articles for a German newspaper and that they had paid him an enormous sum of money in advance—'

154

She stopped, looking over Peter's shoulder with an expression of pleasure and amusement. He turned to see what had distracted her. Claude was just crossing the gangplank. He was loaded to the eyes with parcels and packages. Peter stood up as he came aboard.

'Phyllis, I want you to meet my brother. Claude, this is Mrs du—This is Phyllis.'

'I'm delighted to meet you,' Phyllis said, without rising. 'I enjoyed your concert in Geneva enormously.'

'Thank you. That's very kind of you.'

Peter detected a certain diffidence in the way the other two greeted each other, as if they were instinctively wary of each other. Claude put his parcels down before shaking hands.

'What have you been doing, buying up the village?'

'Very nearly.' Claude flexed his fingers which were stiff from carrying the heavy bags.

'We're just about to drive into Bournemouth for lunch. Why not join us?'

Claude looked towards Phyllis with a faint smile and shook his head. 'No. Thanks a lot, but I've one or two things I'd like to see to.'

'Please,' Phyllis said, 'We'd love you to come.'

'No really, it's very nice of you both, but—' Claude had begun to pick up his parcels again to take them down to the galley. 'I've got several letters to write and I had an enormous breakfast this morning. I swore I'd skip lunch today.'

'That's nonsense!' Peter told Phyllis. 'He's a half-a-grapefruit man. He's just being tactful. All right, Claude, we'll see you later.'

Phyllis smiled at Claude as Peter took her arm and steered her towards the gangplank. Claude watched them

155

thoughtfully as they walked along the quay towards Peter's Jaguar. Then he went down the steps to the cabin and into the galley.

He had unpacked some of the things and was putting them on the appropriate shelves when Peter came clattering down the steps, breathless, into the cabin.

'Forgot my wallet.'

He opened a drawer in one of the chests and took out his wallet. He shoved it into his pocket and was about to dash up the stairway again when he paused.

'Well, what do you think of her?'

'What?'

Claude snapped out of his reverie, saw his brother's flushed and excited face.

'I said, what do you think of her?'

Taken off guard Claude groped for the right words. 'Oh, she's—better looking than I expected.'

Peter grinned with pleasure and disappeared again.

The Jaguar, with Phyllis once again at the wheel, made short work of the drive into Bournemouth. As the car swished past the parks and tree-covered slopes of the seaside resort Peter was feeling elated.

'You still haven't told me where you're staying.'

'At the moment I'm staying at a small hotel near—Just outside London.'

'Was that Talmadge's idea?'

'Yes. He made me stay in hiding.' Just for a second she took her eyes off the road to glance at him. 'He was frightened that you, or rather George Delta, might contact me. Apparently Delta's under the impression I have information which could be of value to him.'

'Information you got from your husband?'

'Yes.'

156

'And have you?'

'No. I haven't.' She slowed to let a pedestrian negotiate a zebra crossing. 'Peter, I'm sorry I can't tell you the name of my hotel but I promised Talmadge I wouldn't tell anyone where I was staying, not even you.'

'That's all right. I understand. Is he picking you up this afternoon?'

'Yes. At three o'clock. Which turning do I take here?'

'Go right round the roundabout and take the third exit.' He waited till she had completed the manoeuvre and was on the correct road.

'I understand about the secrecy but how am I going to get in touch with you again?'

'When are you going back to London?'

'Probably the day after tomorrow.'

'I'll phone your office first thing on Monday morning.'

'Is that a promise?'

She pulled up as the traffic lights ahead showed red, then she turned and smiled.

'That's a promise.'

'Hello, Peter.' Claude looked up with amusement as Peter breezed into the cabin. The latter was smoking a cigar and was obviously very pleased with life. 'If appearances are anything to go by, the lunch was a success.'

'Very much so. You should have joined us.'

'And made an enemy of you for life?'

Claude put the sheets of music he had been studying into an attaché case and closed it. He took another bite from the bar of fruit and nut chocolate he had been eating.

'Didn't you have anything to eat?'

'I made myself a sandwich and bought a bar of chocolate,' Claude said. 'That's all I wanted. When are you seeing Phyllis again?'

'Next week. She's promised to phone me on Monday morning.' Peter sat down on the other side of the table and nodded at the attaché case. 'Why the case?'

'Oh—I was just going to tell you. It's a damn nuisance but I've got to go up to Scotland. I shall be back on Monday or Tuesday.'

'Are you giving a recital?'

'No. As a matter of fact I'm trying to get out of giving one. But they won't take "no" for an answer.'

'When are you leaving?'

'This afternoon,' Claude said casually.

The ash fell off the end of Peter's cigar but he didn't notice.

'This afternoon?'

'I plan to catch the three fifteen. Perhaps you'd run me to the station?'

'Yes, of course,' Peter said, recovering from his surprise. 'Are you flying up?'

'No, I've managed to get a sleeper. My agent's meeting me at Euston.' Claude swallowed the last of his chocolate and threw the wrapping into the wastepaper basket. 'But tell me about your lunch. What happened?'

'I thought I'd had a pretty tough time during the past few weeks, but believe me, it's nothing compared with what Phyllis has been through.'

'I can believe that,' Claude said seriously.

Peter threw him a sharp look but there was no hint of sarcasm on his face.

'There seems to be little doubt that Norman du Salle had incriminating information about certain people in

158

this country. Important people. Scotland Yard were under the impression that Phyllis had this information and they were frightened she might be abducted.'

Claude nodded. 'By George Delta?'

'Yes.'

'I see. Did Phyllis explain about Harley Street, and what happened in the taxi?'

'Yes. For some time Talmadge laboured under the delusion that I was Delta. Phyllis wasn't convinced of this, so in the end they agreed to test me out. The scene in Harley Street was closely watched by the Special Branch and, fortunately for me, my behaviour convinced them that my interest in Phyllis was, well, purely of a personal nature. Later, at Talmadge's request, she telephoned me and—not to put too fine a point on it—gave me the brush off.'

Claude thought about this for a few moments, his brow crinkling slightly.

'But after Phyllis telephoned you, if I remember rightly—' He broke off at the sound of someone crossing the gangplank. 'It's Mrs Frinton. I think I know what she wants.'

Claude rose quickly in an effort to forestall her but before he could get out from behind the table she had appeared at the cabin door. She was carrying a square parcel and several letters.

'Sorry to disturb you, Mr Matty, but these books arrived by the second post. I thought they might be important.'

Peter took the letters and the parcel, which contained some books he was expecting.

'Thank you, Mrs Frinton. That's very kind of you.' She acknowledged his thanks with a friendly nod, then turned to Claude with the respectful smile she reserved for him.

'And your phone call was three pounds forty, sir. I checked with the operator.'

'Oh—thank you, Mrs Frinton.' With a certain embarrassment Claude took three notes from his wallet and felt in his pocket for the necessary silver.

'Three pounds and forty pence.'

'Thank you, sir.' Mrs Frinton received the money on the palm of her hand, her shrewd eyes checking the amount carefully.

'Thank *you*, Mrs Frinton.'

She folded the coins up inside the notes and stowed the little packet into a pocket stitched to the front of her skirt. She embraced them both in her parting smile and departed busily up the steps onto the deck.

'Three pounds forty!' Peter remarked thoughtfully. 'That must have been quite a phone call.'

'Yes.' Claude agreed blandly. 'It was to Scotland. I was talking for ages.'

'You must have been.'

Everything was against Peter that Monday morning. Traffic was being diverted round the centre of London and there were long tail-backs on all the routes to Russell Square. He had to admit that there was force in Mollie Stafford's argument. She was always telling him that he was mad to come by car when the Underground was available. But he liked to have the car on hand, as he so often made trips out of London direct from the office.

To make things worse all the parking meters near his office were taken. He had to leave the car a quarter of a mile away and walk back.

Mollie did not show any surprise at his late arrival. She

160

was becoming used to the pattern. She listened to his excuse with tolerant amusement.

'You should try the Underground. How many times have I told you? There's a pile of letters on your desk and at least half a dozen people have telephoned.'

'I don't suppose Mrs du Salle called?'

'Yes. She did. You've just missed her—by about two minutes.'

'Damn! Is she ringing back?'

'No.' She saw Peter purse his lips in exasperation. 'She phoned to ask you to have lunch with her.'

'Damn! Damn!'

Mollie's face was expressionless as she tore a sheet off her message pad. 'I said you were free.' She handed him the sheet. 'That's the name of the restaurant. One o'clock.'

Peter's face was transformed by a smile of delight. 'Mollie, you're a treasure!'

'And Mr Lerner's been trying to get hold of you,' she called, as he went into his office. 'He's rung twice already.'

'Is he in London?'

'I think so. I didn't ask him.'

'Did he say what he wanted?'

'No. He's going to ring you back.'

He went into his office to hang his coat up but was back in a few seconds.

'I suppose there hasn't been a call from Scotland?'

'Scotland?'

'From my brother. He said he'd let me know when he's coming back.'

'No.' Mollie was shaking her head as the telephone on her desk began to ring. 'I'm afraid there hasn't.' She picked the receiver up. 'Matty Books, can I help

161

you? . . . Just a moment, Mr Lerner, I'll see if he has arrived.'

She covered the mouthpiece with her hand and by dumb-show indicated that he was to take the call in his office. Peter took his time about getting round behind his desk. After the way Max Lerner had treated him he was in no hurry to talk to him.

'Good morning, Max,' he said, polite but frosty. 'This is a surprise. I thought you'd have gone by now.'

'No, I'm still here. I'd like to see you, Peter. Could we have lunch together?'

Max's voice had lost all its bounciness. His tone was almost pleading.

'Today? I'm sorry, that's not possible.'

'Well, could you drop in some time? This afternoon, perhaps?'

'I'm sorry, Max, I—'

'What about this evening?'

'I've got a very busy day, Max.' Perhaps Max had changed his mind, regretted handing the cheque back, but Peter did not intend to give him a second chance. 'This evening I'm due to—'

'Look, Peter,' Max cut in more desperately. 'This is important. I've simply got to see you some time today.'

'Important to you or to me?'

'Important to both of us. I'm not trying to borrow money, Peter. It's got nothing to do with money, I assure you.'

'Then what is it you want to see me about?'

There was a pause before Max answered. When he did so he kept his voice low, as if he feared that someone might be eavesdropping on the conversation.

'I want to talk to you about George Delta.'

'George Delta? Do you know him?'

'Yes, I know him. Peter, I've got to see you!'

Peter hesitated for only a few seconds. 'All right. I'll call round this evening. About eight o'clock.'

For the second time the waiter came to the table with the coffee.

'More coffee, madam?'

Phyllis shook her head.

'Sir?'

'Yes, please. Phyllis, what about a liqueur?'

She declined again.

'You don't mind if I smoke?'

As the waiter departed he lit the cigar he had ordered. He had not wanted to spoil their lunch together by bringing up certain questions but he was beginning to run out of time. There were some questions he desperately wanted the answers to.

'Phyllis, you remember the night I came to the Connaught Hotel—the night we had a drink together?'

'Yes.' She smiled. 'You turned up uninvited.'

'Amongst other things we talked about a man called Max Lerner.'

'Did we? I don't remember.'

'He's a journalist. He was with me the morning I accosted you in the traffic jam.'

'I remember now. He was in the taxi with you.'

'That's right. That's the chap. You said you'd met him.'

'Yes. I met him with my husband, a long time ago—' Her smile had vanished. She looked puzzled. 'I thought I'd told you this.'

'Where did you meet him?'

'In Washington.'

'He doesn't remember meeting you.'

'He doesn't? Well—perhaps I'm mistaken. Perhaps I'm thinking of someone else. But I don't think I am.'

'No. I don't think so either.'

'But why are you interested in this man?'

As he had feared, his reference to the past had dispelled the sense of intimacy which he had felt growing between them during the meal.

'He's done a certain amount of work for me over the years—mostly research work. And he wrote a very good book which we published about five years ago. But tell me what you know about him, Phyllis.'

'I don't know anything about him.'

'But you say you met him in Washington? Where exactly?'

'Oh dear.' She frowned with the effort to remember. 'I think it was at a party. I seem to remember one of the newspapers gave a party to celebrate something or other and this Max—What did you say his other name was?'

'Lerner.'

'Max Lerner. He was introduced to me by my husband, I think.'

'Was he a friend of your husband's?'

'No, I don't think so. In fact, I'm sure he wasn't.' She looked at him with a slight frown. 'But you still haven't told me why you're so interested in him.'

'He telephoned me this morning and said he wanted to see me. He said it was important that we met some time today. When I asked him what he wanted to see me about he said—"George Delta".'

'George Delta?' she echoed, surprised.

Peter nodded.

'Does he know Delta?'

'Yes. At least, he says he does.'

She studied him, still with that slight frown on her face.

'Have you told Talmadge about this?'

'No, I haven't.'

'You should have done, Peter. I think he ought to know about this phone call. I really do.'

'I was going to telephone him, in fact I started to do so, then at the very last moment I changed my mind.'

'Why?'

'I thought perhaps I ought to see Max first and listen to what he's got to say. Perhaps I was wrong. I don't know. Anyway, I'll phone Talmadge tonight.'

'When are you seeing this man?'

'This evening.'

'Where?'

'At his flat.'

'Alone?'

'Yes.' Imperceptibly their tones were reversed. Now it was she who was asking the questions. 'Why do you ask?'

'Perhaps we could meet later, after you've seen him? I'd like to know what happens.'

'Yes, of course. I'll meet you at the—No, wait a minute. That's not a very good idea. I'm seeing him at eight o'clock but I'm not sure how long I'll be with him. Perhaps it would be better if you came to my flat?'

To his surprise she accepted his suggestion after only the slightest hesitation.

'Yes, all right.'

'I'll give you a key in case you get there first and you can let yourself in.' He took one of his business cards from his wallet and wrote his private address on the back. 'Here's the address, it's very easy to find. I'm on the first floor.'

13

It was obvious that Screaming Henry Higgins was bringing plenty of business to the Victorian pub on the corner near Max Lerner's flat; there were no parking spaces in the side street where Peter usually left his car. As he cruised slowly along he saw out of the corner of his eye a woman unlocking the door of a red Metro. She was wearing a shiny black mackintosh and a head scarf. He turned quickly in the next available opening and was behind the Metro as it pulled away rapidly, racing to catch the traffic lights at the junction with Islington High Street before they turned red.

At the entrance to the block of flats he paused to press the button alongside Max's name on the entry-phone panel. After a short delay a man's voice, distorted by the loud-speaker, answered briefly, 'Hello.'

'It's me, Max. I'm coming up.'

The lift had at last been repaired. Perhaps that was a good omen. What had happened on his last two visits had not disposed Peter to trust Max. Nor was he quite convinced that he had been mistaken about the driver of the Triumph Spitfire that evening when his flat had been searched.

The obvious concern which Phyllis had shown about him coming to Max's flat alone had made him more aware that there might be an element of danger. He was glad that at least one person knew he had a rendezvous with Max at eight this evening. It was a kind of insurance.

Rock music still resounded from the flat next to Max's. It seemed to be a permanent feature of the place. Just as he pressed the bell beside Max's door he noticed that there was a Yale key in the lock. As no one came immediately to answer his ring he assumed that Max had left it there so that he could let himself in.

He turned the key and pushed the door open.

He froze.

Max's body was lying on the rug directly under the hall light. His eyes were wide open but fixed and sightless. His mouth gaped, as if the bullet which killed him had silenced a cry of fear or protest. His hands clutched at the ornamental rug. Blood from the wound on his chest was oozing out, spreading a stain that was still widening.

Further along the corridor a door chain rattled and a key grated in its lock. Peter quickly moved into the hall. He pushed the door shut behind him.

That voice which had answered the entry-phone! It had been too blurred for him to recognise. Had Max been killed since Peter had arrived at the entrance downstairs? Or had his killer calmly answered the entry-phone?

Warily he stepped forward, avoiding the pool of blood, and knelt beside Max to see if there was any vestige of life.

Uncannily, the cigar which Max had been smoking had escaped from his fingers and lay near his right hand, still smoking. The scent of tobacco mingled with the tang of cordite.

He was about to straighten up when the door of the sitting room slowly began to open. At first all he saw was a pair of shoes and the bottom half of a pair of trousers. Then his eyes lifted, took in the familiar light overcoat, the casually knotted silk scarf, the gloved hands.

Claude was gripping an automatic in his right hand. It was aimed at Peter.

'Claude! What the hell are you doing here?'

The gun was lowered. 'I'll explain later.'

'Explain now!' Peter demanded, the fright he had received expressing itself in anger. 'He's dead!'

'I know.'

'Then what—'

'I'll explain when Talmadge gets here.'

'Talmadge?' Peter got up off his knees. None of this made any sense. 'You've sent for the police?'

'Yes, of course I have. Good God, Peter, surely you don't think I had anything to do with this?' He waved the gun at the body. 'You don't think I killed him?'

'What are you doing with that gun then?'

'I found it lying in the sitting room. When you phoned from down below I didn't recognise your voice. I only knew that someone was coming up to the flat and I was here alone with a dead body.'

From the street below came the sound of a police car's siren blasting its way through the evening traffic.

Talmadge had brought a murder squad with him, headed by Inspector Holroyd. After the briefest of interrogations Peter and Claude were sequestered with a detective-constable in Max's bedroom while the half dozen specialists who had arrived in Holroyd's wake went about their work. It was not till the sitting room had been photographed, finger-printed and searched that they were brought out to face a more prolonged interrogation. The body had been removed from the hall but there was still activity beyond the closed door.

'You say you had an appointment with Mr Lerner?' Holroyd asked Peter, when they were all seated. Claude and Peter were together on the bearskin-covered settee where Max had made so many of his conquests. Holroyd was a sharp-featured man in his mid-thirties. Whereas Talmadge was confident and suave in his manner, Holroyd was brusque and very much the officer on duty. Peter suspected that his officious manner was intended to impress Talmadge.

'Did he make the appointment, sir?'

'Yes, he did.'

'When?' Holroyd had pulled a straight chair up to the table on which he had placed his notebook.

'This morning. He telephoned my office. He said he wanted to see me and that the matter was urgent. I arranged to see him here at eight o'clock.'

'What was it he wanted to see you about? Have you any idea?'

'Yes, I have.' Peter glanced at Talmadge, who had settled himself in an easy chair on the flank of the settee. He could watch the brothers' faces as they answered Holroyd's questions.

'It was about a man called George Delta.'

'George Delta?' Talmadge repeated the name quietly.

'Are you sure he said that?' Claude said. 'He wanted to talk to you about George Delta?'

'Yes, I'm quite sure.'

Talmadge remarked, 'You seem surprised, sir.'

'I am surprised,' Claude said. 'Very surprised. And for a good reason. You see I happen to know that Max Lerner and George Delta were in fact one and the same person.'

Claude's statement had surprised all three of his listeners. Holroyd remained silent. It was clear that he was out of his depth here. He left it to Talmadge to pursue this new development.

'Go on, Mr Matty,' Talmadge invited. 'Tell us what else you know.'

Claude spread his fingers out and studied them, as if they could help him to put his facts in order.

'Well, I think perhaps I had better start by telling you what happened to an Italian conductor who I knew. His name was Enrico Muralto. About five weeks ago he committed suicide in Stockholm.'

Holroyd nodded to indicate that he'd read about this in the papers.

'His wife, Eva, was a great friend of mine. Like everyone else she was deeply distressed and indeed mystified by her husband's death. Though I must admit that at the time there were strong rumours that Enrico was being black-mailed. After her husband's death I stayed with Eva for two or three days, helping her to sort out various documents. During the course of this we came across a photograph. The photograph puzzled Eva because she'd never seen it before, and, apart from Enrico, the people in the snapshot were completely unknown to her.'

Claude looked from Holroyd to Talmadge. If either of them was wondering how intimate he was with the dead conductor's wife their faces did not show it.

'Go on, Mr Matty,' Talmadge prompted again.

'Three days ago I made a sudden decision. I wanted to take another look at that photograph. So I contacted Eva and flew out to Rome.'

'Rome?'

'Yes, Peter.' Claude turned from Peter's astonished face to Talmadge. 'I arrived back this evening. The first thing I did was telephone this number.'

He indicated the telephone on its low table. It was an indication of the interest he had aroused in his audience that they all followed his glance, as if the telephone could speak and repeat the conversation.

'Of course he was surprised to receive a call from a complete stranger but when I told him that I was Peter's brother he became curious. I told him that I'd just arrived at London Airport and wanted to see him without delay. That's when he told me that Peter was coming here at eight o'clock.'

'What time was this?' Holroyd asked.

'Soon after my plane landed. About a quarter to seven.'

'Mr Matty, this conversation may be important. Can you tell me as closely as possible what passed between you?'

'I'll try, Inspector,' Claude said. 'He asked me to tell him why I was so anxious to see him. I thought it would make him more disposed to talk to me if I showed my hand a little. I told him that I'd been to Rome and that I'd seen Mrs Muralto.'

'What was his reaction?'

'He was obviously taken aback, but he pretended not to know the name. However, he could not keep that up when I told him that I had a photograph of him with Enrico—Mrs Muralto's husband.'

'What did he say to that? Can you remember his exact words?'

'He said, "What is it you want?" I told him that I was not trying to play his game and blackmail him, if that was what he was thinking. He said, "I didn't blackmail Enrico." When I pressed him he said, "I found out things about him and passed the information on. But I didn't blackmail him. I swear I didn't."'

Talmadge and Holroyd exchanged a smile. Peter could imagine Max's protestations.

'I said it was a distinction I'd like to discuss with him and he reluctantly agreed to see me. "I was going to talk to your brother anyway," he said. "I'll be here all evening."'

'I presume you came direct from the airport, sir?' Holroyd said. 'What time did you get here?'

'I arrived here at about ten minutes to eight. I tried the entry-phone at the entrance below but there was no reply, so I came on up here. The front door was closed and no one answered the bell. I hung around, not quite sure what to do and—'

'Did you hear any movement inside the flat?'

'No. But there was a tremendous din coming from the flat next door. Just as I was turning away I noticed that someone had pushed a key under the door. The rest you know. I found Lerner lying dead in the hall and immediately telephoned Scotland Yard. Five minutes later my brother arrived.'

'I see. Thank you, sir.' There was a hint of scepticism in Holroyd's voice. He gazed thoughtfully at Claude. 'And what about the gun? Where did you find that?'

'I told you. I found it on the floor, near that chair. It was either left there deliberately, or someone dropped it.'

'Is that so?' Holroyd spoke with heavy irony. 'That's interesting.'

'Well, that's only my opinion, of course.'

'You should have left it where it was, sir,' Talmadge said mildly. 'But since you didn't, I'm glad you had the sense to put your gloves on.'

'Yes,' Holroyd added. 'It was lucky you had them with you.'

'I suppose it was. But I frequently wear gloves.' Unruffled by the Inspector's insinuation Claude looked at his hands. 'I have to take care of my hands.'

'Yes, well—you'll have to come down to the station, sir. We shall want to take your fingerprints.'

'Yes, of course. I realise that.'

Holroyd turned to Peter.

'You too, sir.'

'I have an appointment later this evening with Mrs du Salle,' Peter appealed to Talmadge. 'I'd very much like to keep it if possible.'

Talmadge made no comment but he gave a little nod of assent. Holroyd resumed his questioning of Claude.

'When you entered the flat did you see anything or hear anything which aroused your curiosity—apart from the dead man?'

'Yes, I heard what I thought was a door closing and I rushed through into the kitchen. The back door was shut but I immediately looked outside to see if I could see anyone.'

'And did you see anyone?'

'No, I didn't. But I don't think I was mistaken. You see, there's a brass chain on the door and when I entered the kitchen it was moving slightly.'

'Very observant of you, Mr Matty,' Holroyd commented drily.

'I don't think so. It was pretty noticeable.'

'You say you arrived at London Airport this evening?'

'Yes. I was on the British Airways flight from Rome. We landed at six fifteen.'

'And the first thing you did was telephone Mr Lerner?'

'That's right.'

'What happened after you spoke to Mr Lerner?'

'I told you. I jumped in a cab and came straight here.'

'You didn't telephone anyone else?'

'No.'

'Not even your brother?'

'No.'

'Why not? I would have thought that was the obvious thing to have done.'

'It was then a quarter to seven. I knew if Peter kept his appointment I'd be seeing him at eight o'clock anyway, so—' Claude was steady and confident under Holroyd's close questioning, but he appeared to decide now that he'd taken enough from the inspector. He turned to Talmadge. 'Besides, I wanted to see Lerner first. I wanted to question him about the photograph.'

Peter knew his brother well enough to be sure that he was hedging. The way Claude had answered Holroyd's last questions made him sure that he was trying to conceal something. He had assumed that the concealment was from the police and not from him—until Claude's next move.

He put his hand into his pocket and drew out an unsealed plain envelope which he handed to Talmadge. Talmadge took a photograph from the envelope and studied it for a moment. His eyes met Claude's. Then he carefully replaced the photograph in the envelope and put it in his own breast pocket.

14

Peter poured a handful of beans into the coffee grinder and switched it on. The raucous noise drowned the soft music from the stereo in the sitting room. While the beans were being ground he took a couple of liqueur glasses from the cupboard and put them on a small tray beside the bottle of Grand Marnier Claude had brought him from the duty-free shop. He had taken off the jacket of his office suit and put on a more comfortable jacket. His pleasurable anticipation at the thought that he would soon be playing host to Phyllis was marred by the nagging doubts caused by Claude's odd behaviour at Max Lerner's flat.

When he turned the coffee grinder off he heard a foot-step.

'Peter? Are you there?'

He rushed out to find Phyllis standing in the hall. She was wearing a fur coat. She had put her hair up and it was arranged in seemingly casual coils on the top of her head.

He stood staring at her. Dressed for an evening out she looked more attractive than ever. There was a hint of excitement in her eyes. 'You look marvellous!'

'I rang the bell but there was no answer. I wasn't sure you were here.'

'I had the coffee grinder on. Here, let me take your coat.'

As he helped her with her fur coat he said:

'I'm terribly sorry I didn't hear you ring. I didn't get back until a few minutes ago and then I remembered that I hadn't made any coffee.'

'What is it, Peter?' She had been watching him anxiously as he fumbled with the coat-hanger. 'You look worried. Has something happened?'

'Yes. But first let me get you some coffee.'

'No, I don't want any coffee. Tell me, why are you so on edge? What happened this evening?'

He did not answer till he had led her into the sitting room.

'Max Lerner's dead. He's been murdered.'

She put a hand to her throat.

'When?'

'Tonight. Just before I arrived at his flat.'

'You mean—he was actually dead when you got there?'

'Yes. His body was in the hall. He'd been shot.'

She walked towards the mirror above the fireplace, staring at the reflection of her face.

'This is terrible! What a shock it must have been for you! Have the police any idea who did it?'

'I don't know, Phyllis. It's difficult to say—'

She noticed his concern and spun round, angry.

'They surely don't think that you had anything to do with it?'

'No, I don't think so, but—' He shook his head unhappily. 'My brother was there. He was in the flat when I arrived. Apparently he telephoned Max earlier this evening and arranged to see him. At least, that's what he says.'

'That's what he says?' she repeated, surprised by the doubt in his voice. 'Does that mean you don't believe him?'

'I don't know whether to believe him or not. He told the police such an extraordinary story. I find it difficult to—I don't know what to believe, Phyllis.'

'Was your brother a friend of Max Lerner's?'

'No.'

'Then why did he want to see him?'

'It's a good question. And it's one I've been asking myself all evening.'

'You know,' she said with a wry smile. 'I think I will have that coffee after all.'

He went into the kitchenette, put a filter paper into the machine and poured the freshly-ground coffee onto it. He switched on the electric current. The coffee would be ready in five minutes.

When he went back into the sitting room she had sat down in an easy chair and was just putting her black handbag on the arm.

'Three days ago Claude told me he was going up to Scotland on business. It now transpires that he didn't go to Scotland, he went to Rome instead. He went to see a friend of his—a Mrs Muralto.'

She glanced up sharply. 'Mrs Muralto?'

'Yes. Have you heard the name before?'

'Yes, I think I have,' she said slowly, frowning at the carpet. 'Her husband was a conductor. Didn't he commit suicide?'

'That's right.'

Out in the hall the door bell gave two short rings.

'I remember reading about it. It happened in Stockholm.'

'Well, apparently Claude—' He broke off, annoyed at the idea of some uninvited caller intruding on their conversation.

'Are you expecting anyone?'

'No.' He took his head. The bell rang again. With a gesture of annoyance he went to answer it. 'Excuse me.'

Julian Talmadge was standing outside the door, suave and affable as usual.

'Sorry to disturb you, Mr Matty, but—I'd very much like to have a word with you, if possible.'

'Yes, of course,' Peter said, trying not to sound too inhospitable. 'Come along in.'

'Thank you.'

Taking his hat off Talmadge stepped into the hall. Peter did not invite him to remove his raincoat.

'Mrs du Salle is here.'

'Oh, I'm sorry. If I'd known I wouldn't have troubled you.' Talmadge halted, looking contrite. 'I'd have telephoned.'

'That's all right, go ahead.'

Reassured, Talmadge went on into the sitting room.

'Good evening, Mrs du Salle.'

'Good evening.' She smiled at him coolly.

'I'm awfully sorry to disturb you like this, Mr Matty, but it is important.'

'Would you like me to—' Phyllis uncrossed her legs, but Talmadge stretched a hand out to show that he had no objection to her hearing what he had to say.

'No, no, please. Don't go. I'm sure Mr Matty's already told you about this evening?'

'About Mr Lerner? Yes, he has.'

'We were just talking about it,' Peter explained.

'Have you any idea who was responsible, Mr Talmadge?'

'No, we haven't—not yet.' Talmadge faced Peter again. 'But there's been a rather curious development. Mr Matty, tell me, when you spoke to Mr Lerner this morning on the telephone did you say quite definitely that you would be seeing him this evening?'

'Yes, I did.'

'You left no doubt in his mind?'

'No, I don't think so. I'm pretty sure I said I'd drop in about eight o'clock. But why do you ask?'

'It would appear,' Talmadge said with slow emphasis, 'that Mr Lerner was under the impression that you might not "drop in". So he wrote you a letter.'

'A letter?'

'Yes. The letter was registered and sent to this address. It was posted this morning, shortly after he spoke to you on the phone.' He took a small slip of paper from his pocket. 'We found the receipt.'

'But—what's in the letter?'

'Your guess is as good as mine.' Talmadge put the receipt back in his pocket. 'But I shall be surprised, very surprised, if it doesn't contain some interesting information.'

He fixed Peter with his most authoritative expression.

'Anyway, the important thing is this. Don't open the letter, Mr Matty. Get in touch with me the moment it arrives. You understand?'

Peter had got up early after a restless, sleepless night. The previous evening had been very frustrating. He was sure that Phyllis would not have taken such evident trouble about her appearance unless she really cared about him. But the news he'd had to give her about Max Lerner had cast a shadow over everything and Talmadge's unwelcome intrusion had finally wrecked the evening. She had left soon after his arrival. It was tantalising, but he was confident that having come once to his flat she would let herself be persuaded again.

Normally he would have talked to Claude about it, but since that strange conversation in Max's flat he felt that his brother was keeping some secret from him. It created a rift between them. Peter had not insisted when Claude said that he'd be staying at the Savoy, especially as he knew that Phyllis would be coming. They'd parted at the police station and Peter was damned if he'd be the first to make contact.

Nonetheless he hurried to answer the phone when it rang.

'Good morning, Mr Matty. Talmadge here.'

'I'm sorry. The post hasn't arrived yet.'

'I know it hasn't. Not to worry. It will. Is your brother with you?'

'No.'

'Are you expecting him?'

'Not in the immediate future.'

'I see. So you are alone?'

'Yes,' Peter said, 'I'm alone.'

'Then please get a chair and sit down. I want to talk to you.'

'That's all right, go ahead.'

'Get the chair, Mr Matty,' Talmadge insisted quietly. 'I think you're going to need it.'

Five minutes later Peter put the phone down. He was not sorry that Talmadge had suggested that he should sit down to hear his news. He was shocked enough to feel physically ill. The door bell had been ringing for a full minute before he dragged himself to his feet and went to open the door.

'Morning, sir,' the postman said, friendlily. 'Registered letter. Sign here, please.'

He thrust the receipt form and his own biro at Peter, who signed quickly.

'Ta. Just the one this morning. No bills.'

Whistling cheerfully he went back towards the stair well. Peter closed the door. He looked at his watch. The time was eight thirteen.

The package was a standard Post Office registered envelope. Its thickness indicated that it contained a considerable wad of documents. The address had been typewritten.

Holding it in one hand Peter went back to the sitting room. He went to his drinks cupboard, the lock of which had still not been repaired. He poured himself a shot of brandy and knocked it back. The bite of the neat liquid coursing down his throat braced him.

He went to turn on the radio component in his music centre. It was tuned to Radio 4. The commentator was reviewing England's prospects in the forthcoming series of Test Matches. Peter sat down in his favourite chair, with his back to the door. He knew that he would not have long to wait. He placed the envelope on his lap and drew the left-hand sleeve of his jacket back so that he could see the face of his watch.

He did not hear her enter the flat. The faintest of sounds behind him told him that she was standing just inside the sitting room door.

Holding the letter he stood up and turned round.

She was wearing the shiny black mackintosh. Her hair had been pulled back and knotted at the nape of her neck. There was no make-up on her face. The automatic in her right hand had a heavy cylindrical silencer fitted to it. The gun, aimed at his stomach, was rock steady.

'Hello, Phyllis,' Peter managed to keep his voice level. 'I've been expecting you.'

She had anticipated total astonishment, but her failure to surprise him only made her more urgent.

'Then you know why I've come. Give me the letter!'

'You shall have it. All in good time. But first, we talk.'

'I didn't come here to talk. Give it to me.'

'What happened the night your husband disappeared?' Bitterness and anger made his voice hard. 'Did he find out the truth about you? Did he find out that you'd been blackmailing his friends? Or were you both in it together—'

'That's enough!' she cut in tersely. 'You saw what happened to Max. Give me the letter.'

In the background the radio commentator had moved on to the county cricket scene.

'Claude thought he had seen you somewhere before,' Peter said, playing for time. 'That's why he went to Rome. He'd seen a photograph of you with Enrico and Max.'

As he moved round the table she tensed, leaning forward. The barrel of the silencer followed in.

'You don't think I'm serious? You think I won't use this?'

It was extraordinary that one human face could express two such completely different characters. The features were the same, as beautiful as ever, but the laughing girl who had beguiled him on the aircraft from Geneva had vanished. The eyes that stared into his were ruthless. Most dangerous of all, there was a hint of panic in them.

183

'After what happened to Linda Braithwaite and Max Lerner, I'm quite sure you'd use it, my dear.'

'Then give me the letter.' She said it with slow menace. As he took a step forward, she warned, 'Don't come too close.'

He held out his arm at full length, only too aware that her finger was tightening on the trigger. She stretched out her left hand, still covering him, and snatched the letter. Without taking her eyes off him she put it under her right arm, then felt in the pocket of the mackintosh.

'Here's your door key. I'd like to keep it as a souvenir but I don't think I'll be coming here again.'

Disarmed by what he took for sincere regret and a brief return of the smile he had found so attractive, he put out his hand for the key. Just as he was about to take it her fingers lost their hold and the key fell to the ground. Instinctively he stooped to recover it. As he did so she raised the gun and brought the heavy silencer down on the back of his head.

Phyllis moved quickly. She put the envelope inside her mackintosh and fastened another button to secure it. She went to the telephone and with a savage jerk ripped the cord from its socket. She unscrewed the silencer from the gun, shoved the automatic in one pocket and the silencer in the other. Then she walked quickly through the hall to the front door. As she left, the sports commentator was previewing the forthcoming athletics meeting at Crystal Palace.

The corridor and stair well were deserted. Rather than wait for the lift she ran down the four flights of stairs to the entrance hall. Her red Metro was parked on the near side twenty yards away. She had left it unlocked. Sloane Court appeared deserted, apart from a milkman making deliveries from an electric float.

In the car she hesitated before putting the key in the ignition. The temptation to see what was in the envelope was too strong. It would only take a few seconds. She pulled out the envelope and ripped it open. She drew out the wad of A4 sheets folded in two. Quickly rifling through them she saw to her horror that every one was blank. Realisation that she had been tricked was instantaneous. She flung the useless sheets onto the passenger's seat and started the engine.

With the power unit revving she accelerated hard towards the Royal Hospital Road end of the street. She was fifty yards from the intersection when a police car slid into view. It stopped, completely blocking her exit from Sloane Court. She braked hard to a standstill. Two uniformed officers climbed out of the car, followed by a sharp-featured man in plain clothes. They were all looking towards her.

She rammed the gear lever into reverse, twisted round and began weaving down the street backwards. She narrowly missed the milkfloat and was half way to the other end when a second police car came round the corner. Knowing that she was trapped she slowly brought the Metro to a halt.

Holroyd and the two officers with him were walking down the middle of the street after her, taking their time. Through the rear window she saw Talmadge climb out of the second car and start towards her.

Talmadge was no coward but as he walked steadily towards the Metro he felt the butterflies swarming in his stomach. He knew that Phyllis was a killer and that she was like a wild-cat cornered. It was virtually certain that she had a gun.

When he was twenty yards away the door of the Metro

opened and she got out. He then saw the automatic in her hand, but he kept steadily on, his eyes fixed on hers. He saw her raise the gun and from the look on her face knew that she was about to shoot. Still he kept going.

He had almost reached the Metro when she suddenly put the barrel of the gun in her mouth.

'No!' Talmadge shouted and flung himself forward.

He was too late. The sound of the shot echoed deafeningly between the houses. Talmadge's face twisted with horror and revulsion as he stared down at the shattered head trailing its bloody knot of auburn hair.

Claude was sitting on a bollard at the quayside of Poole Harbour. It was a warm afternoon. He was enjoying listening to the various agreeable noises which made up the symphony of a small port on a working day. His days of holiday would soon be ending. His agent had persuaded him to give a recital in Monaco the following week and he would have to fit in some practising before then.

The slam of a car door broke into his reverie. He turned round to see a police Rover at a standstill across the roadway. Julian Talmadge had got out and was giving instructions to the driver. As the car moved away Talmadge gave Claude a wave and came towards him.

'Hello, Mr Matty,' Talmadge was in good form and very friendly. 'Nice to see you.'

The two men shook hands. Talmadge was one of those people who expressed good-will with a bone-crushing grip.

'It's good of you to come down,' Claude said, flexing the fingers of his right hand.

'Not at all. You look well, I must say. How's your brother?'

'Physically he's completely recovered, but—well, I suppose no man likes to think he's been made a fool of.'

They started strolling along the quay towards *First Edition*.

'You don't have to tell me that.' Talmadge grinned ruefully. 'I'm afraid I haven't exactly come out of this affair with flying colours.'

'Oh, I wouldn't say that.'

'I would. Unlike my colleague, Mrs Braithwaite, I was taken in by Phyllis du Salle. Utterly and completely. In fact, if you hadn't recognised her, God knows what would have happened.'

Talmadge had shortened his stride to match Claude's, so that the two men were walking in step. Unconsciously the man from the Special Branch had betrayed his military background.

'Well, at the time,' Claude confessed, 'I wasn't a hundred per cent sure. When you enlarged the snapshot there was no doubt.'

'I'm more than grateful for the help you gave us. We all are. Incidentally, you'll be interested to know I've had several conversations with my opposite number in Marseilles. He tells me they never completely believed Phyllis du Salle's story. It's true her husband collected dolls of various nationalities, it was his hobby, but the French have always suspected that their row was about something quite different.'

'You mean, Phyllis invented the story about the doll in the bath to divert suspicion from herself?'

'Yes, and she used the same technique over here. She planted a doll in your brother's flat immediately after Mrs Braithwaite was murdered.'

'But how could she have got into the flat?' Claude

objected, glad to find a loophole in Talmadge's exposé. 'Peter had not given her a key at that time and the lock was not forced.'

'My dear Mr Matty, a trifle like that would not worry the sort of people we've been dealing with. Your brother may not have given Mrs du Salle a key, and he was careful of his own—but Mrs Galloway also had one. We've confirmed that she mislaid her handbag the previous day. It was returned to her through the police. Nothing was missing but of course a copy had been made of the key to the flat.'

'I see,' Claude said, duly chastened for questioning Talmadge's deductions. 'Clever of you to work out that it was Phyllis who planted the doll.'

'I'd dearly like to tell you it was a case of simple deduction on my part. But, alas, it wouldn't be true. Mortimer Brown told me.'

Claude stopped. 'Mortimer Brown?'

'We picked up Brown yesterday afternoon, in Belfast.'

'And he talked?'

'Yes. He didn't have much choice, Mr Matty.' Talmadge's smile boded no good for the photographer. 'We're charging him with the Cassidy murder.'

Peter was in the darkened cabin when Claude brought Talmadge aboard. After the concussion resulting from the vicious blow on the head his doctor had advised him to avoid bright light for a few days. He was pale and tired-looking. Talmadge could tell that he was trying to pull out of a deep depression. Nevertheless, when the Scotland Yard man repeated what he had told Claude there was no mistaking Peter's interest.

'So Phyllis was the principal organiser of the operation?'

Talmadge nodded. 'After she got rid of her husband she

took complete control. She'd been working with him for some time, of course, and she knew most of their contacts. By "contacts" I mean people who supplied them with information and photographs.'

'People like Max Lerner and Mortimer Brown?'

'Yes, and Sir Arnold Wyatt's son-in-law.' Talmadge took a sip from the cup of coffee Claude had set before him. 'Incidentally, I don't know whether you realise it or not, Mr Matty, but she was hoping to find out something about you.'

'About me?'

'Yes, that's why your flat was searched.'

Peter shook his head in bewilderment.

'But tell me, why was the photograph of Phyllis in Mortimer Brown's window?'

'Phyllis had never met Brown and she wanted to make quite sure that he was willing to cooperate with her. Her husband had had trouble with him in the past and she wasn't even sure whether he was prepared to meet her or not. The photograph signified that he was. As soon as Phyllis saw it she telephoned for an appointment.'

'And Brown simply replaced her photograph with the one that had been in the window originally?'

'That's right.' Talmadge nodded with approval, as pleased as a schoolmaster whose pupil has anticipated the answer to a question. As Claude sat down the Scotland Yard man continued talking, happy in his role of elucidator. 'Unfortunately Mrs Cassidy was in the shop when Phyllis telephoned and she overheard part of the conversation. She made up her mind to tell you about it. Brown warned her not to, but she took no notice of him and got in touch with you. The rest you know.'

189

Peter looked at Talmadge thoughtfully. There were still a lot of questions in his mind. But he was not sure that he wanted answers to them. He preferred to go on believing that Phyllis had not been totally false, that she had truly cared for him during those short interludes when he had been so happy in her presence.

'I'm sorry Max was mixed up in all this,' he said. 'I know, strictly speaking, he was no damn good, but—well, in a curious sort of way we were quite fond of each other.'

'He got out of his depth, I'm afraid. That was Mr Lerner's trouble.'

'Why do you think he wanted to see me, the night he was killed?'

'I think he was about to leave the country and was prepared to tell you the whole story. For a price, Mr Matty.'

'Yes.' Peter laughed, but it was a sad laugh. 'Yes, knowing Max, you could be right. Well, I don't know about you two, but I need a drink of something stronger than coffee.'

Peter got up and went to the locker where he kept the brandy purchased on a recent trip to France. Talmadge and Claude exchanged a smile. They were pleased for different reasons; Talmadge because he felt that he had tied the whole case up very neatly. Claude because Peter was at last showing some of his old spirit.

Peter dumped a litre bottle of Rémy Martin and three glasses on the table.

'If you'll forgive me saying so, sir,' Talmadge said, as the cork came out with a plop. 'I think what you really need is a holiday.'

'I couldn't agree more,' Claude approved emphatically.

'I'm giving a recital in Monte Carlo at the end of the month and I'm having a devil of a job trying to persuade him to come out with me.'

'I wish someone would try and talk me into going to Monte Carlo.' Talmadge grinned and put his large hand round the generously filled glass. 'Down the hatch!'

The private hire Ford Granada drew up at the Departures entrance to Terminal 1 at Heathrow Airport. The driver jumped out quickly to open the rear door for his two passengers. Claude and Peter were wearing raincoats over the light clothes which people wear when they are leaving chilly Britain and expect to land in a warmer climate.

Claude signalled to one of the porters standing waiting with his trolley and went to supervise the unloading of their suitcases from the boot. Peter waited on the pavement, holding Claude's precious brief-case in which he carried his music.

A London taxi had pulled up behind the Ford Granada. Peter, watching it idly, felt his interest quicken as an extremely pretty girl stepped out. She was alone, and apparently only had hand luggage for she spurned the offer of a porter. By the time she had collected all her things from the back seat of the cab her arms were indeed full. She was attempting to hold onto a travelling case, a passport wallet, a small bouquet of flowers and several magazines and at the same time to pay the taxi driver.

As she reached out to collect her change the wallet nearly slipped from her fingers. In an attempt to retrieve it she dropped the bouquet. The magazines slithered from under her arm.

Even as she stopped to pick them up Peter was moving to her aid. She straightened up, smiling gratefully as he collected the magazines. He was answering her smile and was about to return the bouquet to her when he felt his arm seized firmly from behind. He turned to find Claude at his elbow. Without a word and with an expressionless face Claude took the bouquet from him and handed it to the astonished girl.

Then, gently but firmly, he led Peter into the airport building.